METAL
MUSIC
A HISTORY FOR HEADBANGERS

THE MUSIC LIBRARY

By Nicole Horning

LUCENT
PRESS

Published in 2019 by
Lucent Press, an Imprint of Greenhaven Publishing, LLC
353 3rd Avenue
Suite 255
New York, NY 10010

Designer: Deanna Paternostro
Editor: Jennifer Lombardo

Library of Congress Cataloging-in-Publication Data

Names: Horning, Nicole, author.
Title: Metal music : a history for headbangers / Nicole Horning.
Description: New York : Lucent Press, [2019] | Series: The music library |
  Includes bibliographical references and index.
Identifiers: LCCN 2018025738 (print) | LCCN 2018026035 (ebook) | ISBN
  9781534565272 (eBook) | ISBN 9781534565265 (library bound book) | ISBN
  9781534565258 (pbk. book)
Subjects: LCSH: Heavy metal (Music)–History and criticism.
Classification: LCC ML3534 (ebook) | LCC ML3534 .H684 2019 (print) | DDC
  781.66–dc23
LC record available at https://lccn.loc.gov/2018025738

Printed in the United States of America

CPSIA compliance information: Batch #BW19KL: For further information contact Greenhaven Publishing LLC, New York, New York at 1-844-317-7404.

Please visit our website, www.greenhavenpublishing.com. For a free color catalog of all our high-quality books, call toll free 1-844-317-7404 or fax 1-844-317-7405.

Table of
Contents

Foreword

Music has a unique ability to speak to people on a deeply personal level and to bring people together. Whether it is experienced through playing a favorite song on a smartphone or at a live concert surrounded by thousands of screaming fans, music creates a powerful connection that sends songs to the top of the charts and artists to the heights of fame.

Music history traces the evolution of those songs and artists. Each generation of musicians builds on the one that came before, and a strong understanding of the artists of the past can help inspire the musical superstars of the future to continue to push boundaries and break new ground.

A closer look at the history of a musical genre also reveals its impact on culture and world events. Music has inspired social change and ignited cultural revolutions. It does more than simply reflect the world; it helps to shape the world.

Music is often considered a universal language. A great song or album speaks to people regardless of age, race, economic status, or nationality. Music from various artists, genres, countries, and time periods might seem completely different at first, but certain themes can be found in all kinds of music: love and loss, success and failure, and life and death. In discovering these similarities, music fans are able to see how many things we all have in common.

Each style of music has its own story, and those stories are filled with colorful characters, shocking events, and songs with true staying power. The Music Library presents those stories to readers with the help of those who know the stories best—music critics, historians, and artists. Annotated quotes by these experts give readers an inside look at a wide variety of musical styles—from early hip-hop and classic country to today's chart-topping pop hits and indie rock favorites. Readers with a passion for music—whether they are headbangers or lovers of

Latin music—will discover fun facts about their favorite artists and gain a deeper appreciation for how those artists were influenced by the ones who paved the way in the past.

The Music Library is also designed to serve as an accessible introduction to unfamiliar genres. Suggestions for additional books and websites to explore for more information inspire readers to dive even further into the topics, and the essential albums in each genre are compiled for superfans and new listeners to enjoy. Photographs of some of music's biggest names of the past and present fill the pages, placing readers in the middle of music history.

All music tells a story. Those stories connect people from different places, cultures, and time periods. In understanding the history of the stories told through music, readers discover an exciting way of looking at the past and develop a deeper appreciation for different voices.

Vivaldi to Vietnam:
Metal's Roots

Metal is a relatively new music genre that did not really come onto the music scene until the 1970s. At that time, disco and pop music were popular; metal was created by artists who wanted to do something different and express their displeasure with society. By this time, the Vietnam War had been going on for many years, and there were many people who had wanted it to end years before. In addition, they did not feel that pop music by artists such as the Beatles, the Beach Boys, and Elvis accurately portrayed the feelings of many people. Out of this situation, Ozzy Osbourne and Black Sabbath were created, and history was made.

Controversy in the Genre

Metal has been largely dismissed throughout history as being simplistic. In fact,

historians and critics of popular music have so far failed to take seriously the accomplishments of heavy metal musicians. The prevailing stereotype portrays metal guitarists as primitive and noisy; virtuosity [skill], if it is noticed at all, is usually dismissed as "pyrotechnics" … Nor are metal's musical accomplishments acknowledged in the reports of the general press, where the performances of heavy metal musicians are invariably reduced to spectacle, their musical aspects represented as technically crude and devoid of musical interest.[1]

Metal has also had plenty of controversy. Whereas pop music created controversy about sexuality—including Elvis's pelvic-thrusting dancing that only allowed him to be shown from the waist up on television and the skin-baring outfits of pop stars such as Britney Spears and Christina Aguilera—metal music was blamed for crime, violence, and suicide. As a result, a war was waged in the 1980s against the genre,

The PMRC believed that certain music had messages that were damaging to listeners. Metal music, especially, was called out during this time. Shown here is the PMRC testifying that music should be labeled based on the lyric content.

headed by Tipper Gore, wife of then-Senator Al Gore. The Parents Music Resource Center (PMRC), an organization created by Gore and other senators' wives, spread the belief that certain music had messages that were damaging to listeners. The senators' wives supported "government labeling of records they deemed threatening to the hearts, minds, morals, and/or eternal souls of American youth."[2] Multiple types of music were targeted—for instance, country artist John Denver received criticism for songs the PMRC thought were about drug use but were actually about spending time outdoors—but metal music featured most heavily in the PMRC's debates.

Crimes that metal fans— sometimes known as headbangers— committed added to the genre's controversy. In the 1980s, metal ended up being linked with a self-professed Satanist, or devil worshipper, who murdered his friend. In addition, talk show host Geraldo Rivera aired a special right before Halloween in 1988 in which he talked about heavy metal lyrics, particularly those in Iron Maiden's album *The Number of the*

Beast. Throughout the 1980s, it was believed that there were secret messages that encouraged violence hidden in metal music. People had this fear because of criminals such as Charles Manson, who ordered the murder of several people in the late 1960s. He claimed there were messages encouraging these murders hidden in music of the Beatles, particularly on their self-titled album that is often called "The White Album." However,

there was no evidence that heavy metal's exploration of madness and horror caused, rather than articulated, these social ills [such as crime, violence, and suicide]. The genre's lyrics and imagery have long addressed a wide range of topics, and its music has always been more varied and virtuosic than critics like to admit.[3]

In other words, rather than causing crime and violence, metal artists were singing about events that were already happening in the world and

that often went unnoticed by others.

A Work of Art

What many outsiders view as a simplistic genre has proved to have staying power. This is because it is not as simple as people think; artists in the genre often create mind-bending songs that can only be clas-

Classical composers such as Johann Sebastian Bach greatly influenced metal music and the complexity of its composition.

sified as works of art. Metal has been influenced by classical music, which can be heard on songs that feature instruments such as violins. Classical composers such as Johann Sebastian Bach and Antonio Vivaldi had a huge influence on metal artists. As Robert Walser wrote in the book *Running with the Devil: Power, Gender, and Madness in Heavy Metal Music,*

> *heavy metal guitarists, like all other innovative musicians, create new sounds by drawing on the power of the old and fusing together their … resources into compelling new combinations. Heavy metal musicians recognize affinities between their work and the tonal sequences of Vivaldi, the melodic imagination of Bach, the virtuosity of Liszt and Paganini. Metal musicians have revitalized eighteenth- and nineteenth-century music for their mass audience in a striking demonstration of the ingenuity of the popular culture.*[4]

Throughout its history, metal has also split off into multiple subgenres—including hair metal, death metal, metalcore, and thrash metal—some of which largely disappeared as metal music evolved. However, metal as a larger genre is here to stay. The techniques of artists in the metal genre disprove the stereotype that metal is simple, and they also prove that it is not going away.

CHAPTER ONE

Evolution of
Early Metal

The end of the 1960s was a time of transition. The Beatles were on the verge of breaking up. Elvis was still making music, but his public appearances and hit songs were rare. The Woodstock music festival occurred in August 1969 and popularized the image of peace and love that is often associated with the late 1960s and early 1970s. Happy pop music and flower power were the fads of the decade—but certain bands were not going to take it. This was also the time of the Vietnam War, which had been going on for many years and would continue to go on for many more. The music may have been happy, but it was not truly expressing how many people felt. One band got tired of that and changed music forever. That band was Black Sabbath.

Bringing "Things Down to Reality"

In the early 1960s, there was an explosion of pop music. Bands from around the world created upbeat, happy pop music that earned the attention of millions of fans. The Beatles arrived in America and brought with them a fan hysteria that was coined Beatlemania. Elvis also arrived on the scene and became a controversial teen idol, loved by young adults for his music and looks, but criticized for his sexual dancing style. During the 1960s, the Who, the Jimi Hendrix Experience, and the Rolling Stones also emerged, creating the third generation of rock and roll. They experimented with heavier drums, distorted guitars, and bass lines that pushed the boundaries of what music was at the time. People had been listening to light songs such as the Beatles' "I Want to Hold Your Hand" or Elvis's "All Shook Up." The Rolling Stones' "Paint It Black" and the Jimi Hendrix Experience's "Voodoo Child" brought music to new levels. These bands were responsible for hard rock music and its typical model—loud, rebellious,

THE VIETNAM WAR

Metal music in the 1960s was largely created because of the Vietnam War and general displeasure with how it was being handled. The war (which the Vietnamese call the American War) lasted from 1954 to 1975. It was a conflict between Communist North Vietnam and its South Vietnamese allies, the Viet Cong, against South Vietnam's government and the United States. North Vietnam's goal was to unify the country into a single Communist government, but South Vietnam wanted a government that was closer to the democratic model of government in the West. U.S. military advisers were in Vietnam starting in the 1950s, but the American military presence increased over time until by 1965, there were more than 500,000 military personnel in Vietnam.

The Vietnam War had a major impact on America. Many people believed the United States should not have become involved in the other country's affairs, and there were many protests against the war. In addition, there were not enough volunteers willing to join the military in the middle of a long, drawn-out war, and the United States instituted the draft lottery. Young men were given a random number between 1 and 366, which corresponded with their birthday, and lower numbers were drafted first. These men would then be required to join the military—unless they dodged the draft, which more than 500,000 men did during this time by running away to other countries, such as Canada. This was a huge change from past wars, such as World War I and World War II, in which the majority of people proudly supported the war and hoped for a chance to serve in the military.

The anti-war sentiment was high in the United States and across the world. Soldiers fighting in Vietnam were not only dying, they were also deteriorating in other ways; many experienced post-traumatic stress disorder (PTSD), which led some of them to drug and alcohol abuse in an attempt to numb their emotional pain. In turn, anti-war protests were held on many college campuses, in major cities, and even during the Democratic National Convention. The extremely long war in Vietnam wore down people around the world. Eventually, the large number of casualties and the growing cost of the war led to the U.S. military being withdrawn by 1973, and South Vietnam fell to North Vietnam in 1975.

dangerous, and unpredictable. These rock bands

provided the soundtrack for a generation [increasingly] disaffected by social injustice and the escalating war in Vietnam. What differentiated these acts from their predecessors was technological advances that enabled new *heights in sonic disruption [such as Blue Cheer's "Summertime Blues"]. These acts were markedly louder not only in volume, but in weaving of brutally blunt social commentary into their lyrics.*[5]

With these bands, new music began to emerge and voice the dark turn the world was taking with current events. Instead of the happy pop music that was an escape for listeners, metal music reflected on the troubling times, forcing listeners to face it. John "Ozzy" Osbourne

thought to himself, What's all this flower [stuff]? I got no shoes on my feet. Taking a trip to a magic land full of peace, love, and sunshine seemed as realistic to Osbourne as taking a trip to Mars. The world was taking a dark turn at the end of the '60s, and the music began to reflect that. "We got sick and tired of all the … love your brother and flower power forever," said Osbourne. "We brought things down to reality."[6]

Black Sabbath: The Beginning

Ozzy had no idea he would be making history in 1967 when Black Sabbath formed. All the original members—Osbourne, Terry "Geezer" Butler, Bill Ward, and Tony Iommi—grew up in Aston, a ward (similar to an American county) of Birmingham in England. They all had working-class families, and the area they lived in was one that was heavily bombed during World War II, which lasted from 1939 to 1945. Even more than 20 years after the end of the war, the area was still struggling to recover from the war and build itself up again. Therefore, the flower power of the 1960s and happy pop music did not resonate with Osbourne and the other members of Black Sabbath. They lived in a struggling town that was made up mostly of people who worked in factories—they were resilient but did not feel the same peace, love, and happiness that others did. On top of that, while it was not in Aston, the war in Vietnam wore on a lot of people during the time. Many did not support the war in Vietnam, and many believed it was not right to fight in it.

According to Ward, there were three options in Aston: join a band, work in a factory, or go to jail. Osbourne was struggling with the last option. His family lived in poverty, and he turned to crime for his family to survive. At one point, he was caught stealing in a clothing store, was fined, and spent six weeks in jail. While in jail, he spent time in solitary confinement for fighting. During his time in jail, though, he decided he wanted to be a singer and make a living making music. When he got out of jail, he put up an advertisement about starting a band and looking for musicians, and guitarist Iommi responded. Even after Iommi got his fingers stuck in a metal pressing machine at the factory he worked at, losing the tips of his middle and ring fingers on his right hand, he did not quit the band. He had to learn how to play guitar all over again; however, this experience made him an incredibly unique guitarist.

Iommi melted pieces of plastic to put over the fingers that got cut so the guitar strings would not damage them further. However, this meant he could not feel the guitar when he played, so he had to relearn the fretboard by listening to the notes. Additionally, the plastic pieces were large and clumsy, so he could not play the guitar quickly. Iommi would have given up if he had not listened to albums by jazz guitarist

Tony Iommi (right) melted plastic to cover his missing finger tips in order to play guitar. The plastic can be seen on the middle and ring fingers of his right hand in this photo.

Django Reinhardt. Reinhardt was paralyzed in one hand with the exception of two fingers. Drawing inspiration from this, Iommi also learned how to play by using only two fingers on his damaged hand. This "helped him develop a number of techniques he might not have discovered otherwise." In addition, it is believed that Iommi "was one of the first guitarists to play just the low strings of a major chord instead of all six strings, which produced the 'power chord.'"[7] With the addition of Ward and Butler, Black Sabbath was officially formed in 1967.

A Dark and Morbid Groundbreaking Sound

As influential as Black Sabbath is in the metal world, much of their music was created in jam sessions, which means the band would get together and just play their instruments without following any plan. David Konow, author of *Bang Your Head: The Rise and Fall of Heavy Metal*, wrote,

[The albums] Black Sabbath, Paranoid, *and* Master of Reality, *were all born from their jam sessions. The band would plod along jamming, then a song would suddenly come together. There was a little arranging done afterward, but for the most part the way* the song was written in the jam session was the way you heard it on the album.[8]

In addition, everything Black Sabbath was doing was completely new. While there are many metal bands for fans to listen to in 2018, with more being created every day, in the late 1960s and early 1970s, Black Sabbath was it. No other music existed that was as dark, loud, and distorted as Black Sabbath's; they were completely unique, and it was all new terrain. As Konow wrote,

Black Sabbath's sound was dark and morbid, more so than any other band at the time. They were one of the first bands to tune their guitars lower, often as much as three semitones, which gave their riffs more depth and texture and could make a single chord sound huge and oppressive. Many metal bands would later tune down their instruments, and the intense levels of volume and distortion at which Black Sabbath played is now standard for every hard rock and metal band.[9]

The sound that influenced a whole new genre was born out of their hometown: Their upbringing in Aston was dark and depressing, and the unique sound that Black Sabbath created would probably not

INFRARED FILM AND AN ICONIC COVER

Black Sabbath's self-titled debut album featured an unsettling image of a woman dressed all in black with a mill in the background. Plenty of rumors surround this famous album image, including that the person in the photo was an actual witch, that it was actually Ozzy wearing women's clothes, and—the best rumor, according to the website Loudwire—"There was no woman at the photo shoot—the ghostly figure only appeared when the film was developed. As fun as the legends are, that's all they are: stories. She was really there, really paid for her day's work, and *might* have been named Louise."[1]

The unsettling cover of Black Sabbath's first album (shown here) spawned many rumors.

The photo was taken by Keith MacMillan, also known as Marcus Keef. Keef took the image using infrared film, which "captures invisible infrared light from the red end of the spectrum, light that's not visible to the naked eye and characteristically turning green vegetation a bright red."[2] This technique is what created the red leaves and grass surrounding the figure in front of the mill, which was built in the 1400s and was located in Oxfordshire, England. Terry "Geezer" Butler said, "The album cover did a brilliant job in representing the music ... The more I saw it, the more I became convinced that it was visually just right. It's haunting, eerie, and a little scary. That's what we were after on the album."[3] Keef later went on to produce music videos for the Who, Paul McCartney, Queen, and more, but his influence on the Black Sabbath album cover set the tone for the band's music and is an iconic work of art even decades after the album was initially released.

1. James Stafford, "Cover Stories: Black Sabbath's Self-Titled Debut," Loudwire, August 5, 2015. loudwire.com/cover-stories-black-sabbath-self-titled-debut/.

2. Tracy Mikulec, "Infrared Photography—Transforming Landscapes into Science Fiction Scenes," The Dark Room, September 27, 2017. thedarkroom.com/infrared-film-photography/.

3. Quoted in Stafford, "Cover Stories: Black Sabbath's Self-Titled Debut."

have come out of somewhere such as California. Ward said,

It just seemed like the right thing to do, to go with those moods ... Emotionally it was very satisfying for everybody, almost healing in a sense. Especially when you're real young and there's a lot of anger. Playing drums with Sabbath is the greatest transport one can have to deal with one's anger.[10]

Forbidden Black Sabbath

As influential as Black Sabbath became, they initially had a hard time getting gigs. They would often go to shows where musician Jeff Beck was performing because he was known for not showing up; if he did not show up, Black Sabbath would take his place. Eventually, the band got a gig at the Marquee Club in London, England. However, getting a record label to sign them was as hard as getting gigs. The band knew that what they were doing was different, but they did not fully realize how different they were until they were trying to get signed to a label. They were met with a lot of resistance and were rejected by 14 record labels before manager Jim Simpson was able to get them a deal with Vertigo.

The band both impressed and stressed out their producers in the studio. They were impressed with the band's proficiency because they did everything in one take, but they were upset that the band would not turn their instruments down. Their producer yelled at them that they could not play at such a loud volume in the studio, and the band responded by telling him that they did not turn their instruments down—only up.

The band expected to release a couple of albums, then go back to working in factories. They were surprised when *Black Sabbath* went to number 8 on the British album charts. The song "Black Sabbath" on the album, which was named for a horror movie that also inspired the band's name, was simple and effective. The song has three chords and is played in a slow, swinging jazz beat with ominous, dark guitars and lyrics. The imagery in the album sleeve of upside down crosses added to the dark, terrifying nature of the band. It also got them accused of witchcraft when they toured in America after releasing their debut album.

Following the popularity of their self-titled debut, the band released *Paranoid* in 1970, which included a song called "War Pigs" about the Vietnam War as well as the famous tracks "Iron Man" and "Paranoid." Black Sabbath quickly became a controversial and forbidden band because of the dark nature of their sound and lyrics. When Metallica's James Hetfield was young, he would

Black Sabbath broke boundaries with their dark, haunting sound that would end up influencing metal bands in the future.

list Black Sabbath as a favorite band when talking to his friends. His friends would then say their mom would not let them even own an album of Black Sabbath's. Hetfield said, "Sabbath was forbidden, not the right thing to do."[11]

Paranoid made Black Sabbath an even more famous band—in the United States, it sold more than 4 million copies, and it went to number 1 in Britain. In 1971, the band released *Master of Reality*, an album that was both written and recorded in only three weeks. This album also included Iommi playing flute, which further broke boundaries and made it even more haunting.

In 1972, the band released *Black Sabbath Vol. 4*. At this point, they were more accepted by fans, but not by critics. In fact, their credit as one of the fundamental bands in metal music did not come until the

1990s, when Kurt Cobain of Nirvana credited them as an influence. However, fans of certain things, whether it is a music genre or movie genre, often embrace what critics dislike. By the late 1970s, Black Sabbath had sold millions of records, and their music would be the standard that metal bands in the future would compare themselves to. At the time, though, the band was starting to fall apart—they were partying a lot under the influence of drugs, and in the late 1970s, Osbourne left the band. Ward and Butler soon followed, and Iommi kept Black Sabbath alive with different musicians in their places.

In 2011, the band announced a reunion, but just a few months after the announcement, Ward backed out. The rest of Black Sabbath carried on with their 2013 album, *13*, and the tour without Ward, using Rage Against the Machine's drummer Brad Wilk on the album and Osbourne's solo drummer Tommy Clufetos on the tour. In 2015, Ward stated he had no plans of reuniting with the band until Osbourne apologized for certain comments he made about Ward. Ward did not clarify what those comments were.

Deep Purple

In 1968, Ritchie Blackmore, Jon Lord, Ian Paice, Ian Gillan, and Roger Glover joined to form the band Deep Purple. Deep Purple shifted their musical focus from rock to metal, and just like Black Sabbath, they were created out of displeasure with the current events of the time. Gillan and Glover were in a typical 1960s flower-power band called Episode Six, but at the end of the 1960s, their music started to become tougher because of the darkness and despair of this time period. Gillan and Glover then joined Deep Purple, and by 1971, they had some of the loudest music in metal—a feat that was even acknowledged in the *Guinness Book of World Records*. According to Konow, "one reason for this was that the band had taken off so fast in America, moving up from clubs to arenas, and they had to buy more amps. When they hauled their giant P.A. system back home to England, they went back to playing smaller theaters yet kept the volume levels the same."[12] Along with this distinction, they also had one of the first keyboard players—Jon Lord. Lord played a Hammond B-3 organ that had a heavy sound, which most metal bands at the time still looked down on because they thought it was wimpy to use a keyboard in metal music. However, many metal bands later used keyboards as well. For example, Mötley Crüe used the same Hammond B-3 organ on their *Shout at the Devil* album.

The band had limited success in 1968, although they did attract attention with the albums *In Rock*

Deep Purple was acknowledged as one of the loudest metal bands by the Guinness Book of World Records.

and *Fireball*. However, it was *Machine Head* that cracked the top 10 in the United States, landing at number 7. The goal with the album was to "create a studio album in a live setting. The band wanted to capture the live energy that's so elusive to nail on record."[13] The band recruited Martin Burch, who would later go on to work on Black Sabbath and Iron Maiden albums, to work on *Machine Head*. One of the most famous songs

in metal on this album was "Smoke on the Water," which was based on a true experience the band had. At a show in Switzerland, someone fired a flare gun inside during the concert. The flare hit the ceiling, causing a fire to spread throughout the building and over a lake nearby. From this terrifying experience, one of the first songs most aspiring guitarists learn was created. The song went to number 4 on the charts, and the album sold 2 million copies. By 1974, the band had sold around 15 million albums, but also around this time, the band started to fall apart. Gillan left the band in 1973, later joining Iommi's version of Black Sabbath. Glover went on to work in music production with bands such as Judas Priest, and other band members went on to solo careers. Deep Purple reunited in 1984 with *Perfect Strangers*, and in 2017, they released their 20th album, *Infinite*.

Judas Priest

In the 1970s, a band emerged that would change the look and sound of metal forever—Judas Priest. Not only did they have the vocal power of Rob Halford, but they also had dual guitarists Glenn Tipton and K. K. Downing—and the goal of being the ultimate metal band.

Downing formed the band with bassist Ian Hill, and in 1971, Halford joined them. In 1974, Judas Priest got both drummer Tipton and a recording contract. They released their first album that same year, but it did not sell well. Neither did 1976's *Sad Wings of Destiny*. In 1977, the band signed with Columbia records and released *Sin After Sin*, which was produced by Deep Purple's Roger Glover. The band developed a following, and the songs brought metal into new territory. As Ian Christe wrote in *Sound of the Beast: The Complete Headbanging History of Heavy Metal,*

nothing before matched the speed of Glenn Tipton and K. K. Downing's guitars or the high drama of Rob Halford's phenomenal voice. Judas Priest skimmed the most intense elements of the past into a cauldron and remixed perception in a magical way. "I was inventing my vocal technique as it went along, really," says Halford. "I didn't really have much in terms of people that sounded cool to look around and say I wanted to sound like this or emulate that."[14]

While Halford's voice has been widely praised, the overall composition of the instruments has been equally praised. The dual guitars of Downing and Tipton brought Judas Priest's music into an area that was both melodic and rhythmic; it would even change tempo within the same song, going from a breakneck speed to a more reserved pace. Christe wrote,

Judas Priest's music was very formal, tightly organized around breaks, bridges, and dynamic peaks … The melodic, mind-expanding interplay of Tipton and Downing used twin lead guitars as carving tools to deftly cut and shape sound at

high-decibel volumes. Each scorching lead guitar break was inserted in another perfect song crevice, pointing the way to new invulnerable creations.[15]

Judas Priest's lyrical inspiration came from unlikely places—William Shakespeare and Chinese military strategist and writer Sun Tzu, who is credited as the author of *The Art of War*. These lyrics were delivered by Halford's powerful voice. He said, "I was blessed with extraordinary vocal chords that can do some bizarre things … and it was always a case of looking at new ways of doing things from song to song. It was all about experimentation more than anything else."[16]

It took 7 albums for Judas Priest to crack the top 40 on the album charts in the United States. *British Steel* landed at number 34 and is considered a metal-defining album. Well-known songs such as "Breaking the Law" and "Living After Midnight" made the top 20 in Britain. Their 1981 follow-up album did not build on their momentum, but *Screaming for Vengeance* made Judas Priest a hit in the United States, especially with the song "You've Got Another Thing Comin.'"

Judas Priest became as known for their live shows as they were for their actual music. They put on dramatic stage shows that would later be echoed in the live shows of bands such as Avenged Sevenfold, who had a moving deathbat prop (the band's mascot: a human skull with wings) that was the size of the stage behind them. Judas Priest created the "look" of metal with biker-like leather and studs. They built on this biker look with their stage shows, in which they rode actual motorcycles onto the stage. Halford got the idea of entering the stage on bikes for their song "Hell Bent for Leather." However, at the time, the band did not own bikes, so they bribed bikers who came to their show with drinks if they would let them ride their bikes onto the stage. The band did not stop there with their showmanship—they also incorporated flamethrowers, which required the band to memorize which places on the stage to avoid at certain points in order to avoid injury. In addition, on one tour, the band had a robot pick up Tipton and Downing. They aimed to fully entertain fans with their stage shows.

Judas Priest became part of the controversy that has followed metal since its creation. Two Reno, Nevada, teenagers shot themselves in 1985, and it was claimed that a song on Judas Priest's album *Stained Class* made them do it. One teenager died instantly; the other lived

*Judas Priest helped create the look and sound
of metal music, setting trends that other bands later followed.*

but died three years later from a drug overdose. The parents sued Columbia Records and the band for $6.2 million, and Judas Priest was found to be not guilty after a six-week trial in 1990. Halford said of the incident:

It tore us up emotionally hearing someone say to the judge and the cameras that this is a band that creates music that kills young people. We accept that some people don't like heavy metal, but we can't let them convince us that it's negative and destructive. Heavy metal is a friend that gives people great pleasure and enjoyment and helps them through hard times.[17]

In 1992, Halford left the band and was replaced by Tim "Ripper" Owens until 2003, when Halford

MOTÖRHEAD: NOT HEAVY METAL

Motörhead is a band that rejected the heavy metal label that was often placed on them by fans and critics. Lemmy Kilmister, founder and former front man of the band, hated when people said they were heavy metal—he said they were rock and roll. However, without Motörhead, Metallica and several other bands would not exist. In addition, the heavy sound of Motörhead is responsible for the subgenre of thrash metal that emerged in the early 1980s. As Paul Elliott wrote, "the way that Motörhead played rock 'n' roll—fast, bludgeoning, everything louder than everything else—was an inspiration to almost every metal band that followed in their wake."[1]

Motörhead's *Overkill*, *Bomber*, and *Ace of Spades* albums from the late 1970s and early 1980s were especially important to later metal bands. The aggression and speed of Motörhead influenced nearly every thrash metal band, as well as punk and extreme metal bands of the 1980s. Lars Ulrich of Metallica said,

> *I got introduced to Motörhead's music in 1979, when* Overkill *came out. I'd never heard anything like that in my life. The subsequent ride that this music took me on was to a place I'd never been. So when I say that Lemmy is the primary reason I'm in a band, and that Metallica exists because of him, it's no cheap exaggeration.*[2]

Along with the heaviness of Motörhead's music and their distorted bass lines, the attitude of the band members and even their cover art greatly influenced metal. Their debut album featured a beast with tusks, along with the band name in red on a black background. This skull became their mascot and was known as Snaggletooth. Years later, other bands such as Iron Maiden and Avenged Sevenfold would also incorporate a mascot. Even Ozzy Osbourne said Kilmister was his hero— Osbourne knew Kilmister before he even started Motörhead, and Motörhead opened for Osbourne on his first solo tour.

In 2015, the music world got the devastating news of Kilmister's death. Motörhead drummer Mikkey Dee confirmed the band was over because Lemmy was Motörhead and without him, they could not create new music or tour. Many metal artists paid tribute to him, including Ozzy Osbourne, who wrote that without Kilmister, "there's a big hole in the music industry."[3]

1. Paul Elliott, "How Motörhead Influenced Heavy Metal Music," *Metal Hammer*, February 2, 2016. www.loudersound com/features/how-motorhead-influenced-heavy-music.

2. Quoted in Elliott, "How Motörhead Influenced Heavy Metal Music."

3. Quoted in Kory Grow, "Ozzy Osbourne Remembers Lemmy: 'He Was My Hero,'" *Rolling Stone*, December 29, 2015. www.rollingstone.com/music/news/ozzy-osbourne-remembers-lemmy-he-was-my-hero-20151229.

returned. In 2005, they released their *Angel of Retribution* album, followed by *Nostradamus* in 2008. In 2010, they won their first Grammy Award for Best Metal Performance for their song "Dissident Aggressor." The song was originally released on *Sin After Sin* in 1977, and was reissued on a live album. It took more than 30 years for the band to be recognized this way for their impact on metal.

In 2014, they released their 17th album, *Redeemer of Souls*, with Halford, Tipton, Richie Faulkner, Ian Hill, and Scott Travis making up the band. Judas Priest then toured in 2018 to promote their 18th album, *Firepower*. They continue to be a band that is in demand and creating influential metal music decades after their first album.

"Godfather of Heavy Metal Theatrics"

As metal solidified its place in music, stage shows became more theatrical, which is especially seen in the work of Alice Cooper. Cooper is credited as "the godfather of heavy metal theatrics"[18] and has included gallows, guillotines, and sledgehammers as part of his live shows.

Born Vincent Furnier, he loved horror movies since he was a child. He often cheered for the villains, such as Dracula, Frankenstein's monster, King Kong, and Godzilla—this would influence his shocking stage shows later on. Furnier's parents were alarmed by bands such as the Beatles, and it became Furnier's goal to come up with things that would make the Beatles seem tame by comparison. He created a band called Alice Cooper and took the same name for himself.

Guitarist Glen Buxton of the Alice Cooper band started putting dark circles around his eyes by using cigarette ashes, and other members of the band followed with actual black makeup instead of ashes. However, Cooper's look of dripping mascara and black lines above and below his eyes became his trademark and the most famous look. Alice Cooper's band gained a reputation as "the worst band in L.A.,"[19] and some people could not sit through even a few songs at their live shows. However, talent manager Shep Gordon, who had recently graduated from the University at Buffalo in Buffalo, New York, was introduced to the band and was interested. He wanted people to rush in to see them, not rush out away from them. It was hard to find record labels that were as interested in the band as Gordon was, however. During one meeting, Gordon was told that the band could be signed if they got

Alice Cooper made it his goal to shock people with his stage theatrics, which have included snakes, guillotines, electric chairs, gallows, and more.

rid of Furnier, which, of course, was out of the question. Eventually, they received a contract with Frank Zappa's Straight Records, which was looking for shocking musicians. After two unsuccessful albums, the band moved from Los Angeles, California, to Detroit, Michigan in the early 1970s. This move was incredibly important in the band's career because Detroit was where they found acceptance and true fans.

Another pivotal thing happened around this time—Straight Records was sold to Warner Brothers, which was not too happy about acquiring Alice Cooper. Gordon, however, still had faith in the band and believed all they needed was the right producer.

At this point, Bob Ezrin stepped in. With his production work, the band created a clearer sound, and they also crafted popular anthems such as "Eighteen" and "School's

Out." "Eighteen" was released as a single in 1971, and Warner Brothers would only allow Alice Cooper's band to create a whole album if the song did well. It became an instant hit, so the band released the album *Love It to Death*. Around this time, the band started incorporating the theatrics they became known so well for. This included using snakes, an electric chair, and even a sword that Cooper accidentally stabbed his leg with—he continued performing and made it look like it was part of the show.

In 1971, the band released *Killer*, followed by two albums in 1973, one of which was *Billion Dollar Babies*. In 1974, Furnier's identity as Alice Cooper became more well-known than the band as a whole, and he left the band to create his own solo work. In 1975, he released his first solo album, *Welcome to My Nightmare*, and proved that he was more than just theatrics. He continued to release music during and after the 1970s, and he continues to incorporate theatrics into his stage shows. However, at this point, the audience knows they are just for show, so they are no longer afraid of things such as the guillotine onstage. In 2017, Cooper released the album *Paranormal* and was cast as King Herod in NBC's live performance of *Jesus Christ Superstar*.

The Devil's Tritone

Metal music has been accused of being simple. However, metal fans know that in truth, it is actually creative, is complex, and has texture—just like classical music. A favorite chord of metal bands, in particular Black Sabbath, is the tritone, which has also been called the devil's interval, the devil's triad, and *diabolus in musica* in Latin. In 1998, metal band Slayer released an album titled after this Latin phrase.

The tritone is an interval that spans three whole steps, and it is given names such as the devil's interval because it does not feel natural—it feels unfinished. Between the tones of the tritone, there are erratic jumps that the ear picks up on, and it feels as though another chord should follow for resolution. It was labeled as "false music" because it did not have a natural progression. The uncomfortable feeling the tritone gives led to a rule banning it from musical compositions during the Renaissance (a period of exploration of culture, astronomy, philosophy, and art that lasted from the 14th through the 16th centuries). At this time, people believed the purpose of music was to be beautiful and express the greatness of God. Music that had any other purpose was avoided. After the Renaissance ended, music was allowed to express tension, and this musical interval was perfect for that. However, it has also been used in more lighthearted music, such as the theme songs of *The Simpsons* and *South Park*.

The devil's tritone was explored in the music of classical composer Franz Liszt, and Black Sabbath popularized the interval again around 100 years later. The interval gave a creepy and unusual structure to Black Sabbath's music. The band often used anti-Christian imagery, such as the upside down crucifixes on their album cover, but Iommi used the gloomy-sounding interval simply because it sounded right to him for the song—he did not know its history of being banned and the viewpoint of the interval conjuring the devil in the past.

Gathering the Followers

Metal has evolved from hard rock and displeasure with current events, such as war, to a clearer, more composed sound with multiple guitars and mind-bending musicianship. In the late 1970s and 1980s, metal was starting to gather more followers, and the greatest influencer in metal, Ozzy Osbourne, became popular once again for his solo work.

CHAPTER TWO

New Wave of
British Heavy Metal

Early metal had a slight blues influence, but as the genre started to take shape, that influence was largely eliminated and elements from punk music were adopted instead. Called the New Wave of British Heavy Metal (NWOBHM), this resulted in a more aggressive, faster, bombastic sound that was characterized by artists such as Iron Maiden and Saxon. The end of the 1970s put metal music in a slump as the disco craze caught on, but with the NWOBHM, the genre was revived. Just as Judas Priest had taken inspiration from works by William Shakespeare, music in this period was influenced by mythology and fantasy. Artists of the NWOBHM, especially Iron Maiden, continued the trend of elaborate stage shows, but the most important thing to come from this time was the acceptance of metal as a valid music genre rather than just a fad.

Diary of a Madman

Ozzy Osbourne left Black Sabbath after the tour for the band's *Never Say Die* album, which came out in 1978. After divorcing from his first wife, Thelma Mayfair, he met and later married Sharon Arden, who convinced Osbourne to start a solo career. In 1980, *Blizzard of Ozz* was released, and in 1981, it was certified gold by the Recording Industry Association of America (RIAA), which means it sold 500,000 copies. In 1982, it was certified platinum, which means it sold 1 million copies. As of 2018, it has been certified four times multi-platinum with 4 million copies sold. The landmark single from this album that helped catapult its success was "Crazy Train." In 1981, *Blizzard of Ozz* was followed by the equally successful *Diary of a Madman*, which has sold more than 3 million copies. A moment that Osbourne is unfortunately well known for occurred on the tour for this album, when an audience member threw what Osbourne thought was a rubber toy on the stage. He grabbed it, bit it, and soon learned his mistake—he had bitten the head off of a live bat.

Osbourne released *Bark at the Moon* in 1983, *The Ultimate Sin* in 1986, *No Rest for the Wicked* in 1988, and *No More Tears* in 1991. This last album gave Osbourne his first top 40 hit—"Mama, I'm Coming Home"—11 years after starting his solo career. In 1992, he announced he was retiring from the music business, but this lasted only a few months. In 1993, he earned his first Grammy Award for "I Don't Want to Change the World." He released the album *Ozzmosis* in 1995 and then created a music festival that is a must-see for metal fans: *Ozzfest*. Osbourne reunited

Ozzy Osbourne is the one of the most celebrated artists in metal music, with a career that spans five decades. In 2018, he stated he would not be going on world tours anymore.

with Black Sabbath by the end of the 1990s and then starred in the reality TV show *The Osbournes* with his wife, Sharon, and children, Kelly and Jack. The show ran from 2001 to 2005 and was the third-highest rated cable TV show within just a few months of its premiere. Two years after the show ended, Osbourne released his first album in six years, *Black Rain*, followed by *Scream* in 2010.

In February 2018, Osbourne announced a farewell tour called *No More Tours 2*. However, he said he was not retiring; he just did not want to do world tours because he no longer wanted to travel for long periods of time. He stated he would continue to make music and perform on tours that were shorter than six months.

Beginning of the Movement

The NWOBHM began in the 1970s and was characterized by elements of punk music, rock, and a tougher sound. The name was coined by the media, and many successful metal acts came out of this time period. Some of these acts are still successful as late as 2018 and are still touring and making music. The music of the NWOBHM period featured fast guitar solos, power chords, epic vocals, and deeper lyrics. The lyrics of this time took on fantasy themes and mythical meanings and became popular with new audiences. Around this time, fantasy stories such as the *Lord of the Rings* trilogy by J. R. R. Tolkien and the fantasy role-playing game *Dungeons & Dragons* became popular with audiences, which was reflected in heavy metal music. *Dungeons & Dragons* allows players to take on roles as elves, magic users, warriors, and even musicians. The games often revolve around defeating monsters and collecting treasures while working toward a larger heroic goal. As Christe wrote,

much of heavy metal took place on a similar turf, a realm of dark towers and impenetrable wilderness populated by battles and adversity. "You've gotta write about heavy subjects; the metallers freak out over it," Dan Beehler of Exciter told Canada's The New Music television show. "It's better than something like 'I was walking down the street, da da,' you know? The medieval days were heavy; it was certain death for most people. That's what metal's all about—it's a fight."[20]

One of the most celebrated acts to come from the NWOBHM is Iron Maiden. Def Leppard and Saxon also came on the scene during this era, but while Def Leppard's early releases came out during the

NWOBHM, their later releases shifted toward rock. Saxon, meanwhile, continues to release albums, but the band has encountered many struggles in the music business. Iron Maiden, however, is one of the most influential bands in metal music, lasting long after the NWOBHM period died out only a few years after it started.

Iron Maiden

Iron Maiden's metal career has spanned more than four decades; the band formed in the mid-1970s and released their 16th album in 2015. Their first, self-titled album was released in 1980 and, following Motörhead's trend, it features a mascot that has followed them throughout their career. Named Eddie, it is a greenish ghoul that appears on album covers, T-shirts, and more. At this point, MTV still had not been created, and metal received little airplay on the radio. Therefore, one way for a band to be discovered was by a fan picking an album up because it had a cool cover. The album cover art said a lot about what type of music it was, as was shown with Black Sabbath's first album—the fans knew they were not getting soft pop music. Considering the lack of radio airplay, it took a while for Iron Maiden to kick off—in the United States, at least. In Britain, however, their debut album hit the top 5, and their follow-up, *Killers*, hit number 12.

Iron Maiden wrote literate lyrics that distinguished them from other bands in the metal genre. For example, "Murders in the Rue Morgue" on *Killers* was inspired by an Edgar Allan Poe story of the same name. The song "The Number of the Beast" on the album of the same name was inspired by the horror movie *The Omen II*, and "Flight of Icarus" on 1983's *Piece of Mind* was inspired by ancient mythology.

One of their most ambitious songs based on a piece of literature is "Rime of the Ancient Mariner" on the *Powerslave* album. The song, clocking in at more than 13 minutes, is based on the epic poem of the same name by Samuel Taylor Coleridge and tells the tale that is in the epic poem. The song starts with lyrics such as:

Hear the rime of the
  Ancient Mariner
See his eye as he stops one
  of three
Mesmerizes one of the
  wedding guests
Stay here and listen to
  the nightmares
of the sea[21]

However, the ambition in the song goes beyond just summarizing the tale Coleridge wrote. It even

IRON MAIDEN: SETTING THE STANDARD FOR TOURS

It is incredibly important for musicians to have a stage presence and put on a great show. A concert is where a band gets to truly showcase their skills—they want to put on an entertaining show, yet they want to prove that their talent is real and not manufactured in a studio. Iron Maiden is one of the bands of the 1970s and 1980s that created elaborate concerts that complemented the music. Although many bands successfully create shows that are theatrical, no one puts on a show quite like Iron Maiden. Their shows fully immerse fans in the music and in the world the band has created. The band creates the show's setlist and bases the theatrical elements of the show around it, so fans going to multiple shows on one tour may find it does not change much.

In their first shows in the 1970s, they had a giant papier mâché mask of their mascot, Eddie, which squirted fake blood. In 2003, their shows included a wrap-around stage with artwork from previous albums and Eddie printed on a stage curtain above it all. In 2006, the tour theme was the trenches of World War I, and in 2010, the theme was a giant spaceship. In 2016, the stage show included a giant figure of Eddie on the background curtain as well as a person in a giant Mayan-themed Eddie costume walking around the stage. However, one of the most memorable shows Iron Maiden put on, and one that fans and critics praise, was on their 1984 to 1985 tour, in which they recreated the Egyptian themes on their *Powerslave* album artwork. In the back and center of the stage, there was a giant figure of Eddie as an Egyptian pharaoh that would move and be replaced by a giant, moving, mummified Eddie figure. Pyramids and other Egyptian images surrounded the band, and other theatrical elements such as lights and fire were also used during the show.

quotes from it with lines such as:

*Day after day, day after day,
we stuck nor breath nor motion
As idle as a painted ship upon a
painted ocean
Water, water everywhere and
all the boards did shrink
Water, water everywhere nor
any drop to drink*[22]

One of Iron Maiden's most famous songs is "Run to the Hills" on *The Number of the Beast*. This album topped the charts in Britain and catapulted the band to popularity in the United States. It was the first of seven albums in a row that went either gold or platinum. This is even more remarkable considering the fact that there was virtually no exposure for the band

*Iron Maiden is known for putting on elaborate, theatrical concerts.
As technology has advanced, so has their stage show; it always includes plenty
of lights, fire, and Eddie (shown here holding a flag) in some form.*

on MTV or the radio. With *Piece of Mind*, the band started to be recognized on the Billboard charts in the United States, and they stayed there through subsequent releases, including *Powerslave*, *Live After Death*, *Somewhere in Time*, *Seventh Son of a Seventh Son*, *No Prayer for the Dying*, and *Fear of the Dark*. The band further cemented their popularity in the United States with "Bring Your Daughter to the Slaughter" off of *No Prayer for the Dying*, which was originally recorded by vocalist Bruce Dickenson for the *Nightmare on Elm Street 5: The Dream Child* soundtrack.

Members of the band came and went, but the band still continued to tour and create new music, including the albums *The X Factor* in 1995 and *Virtual XI* in 1998.

Iron Maiden is one of the most successful bands to come out of the New Wave of British Heavy Metal era. They have performed thousands of times and sold millions of albums that include songs inspired by works of literature.

Dickinson had left the band but reunited with them in 1999, bringing them back to success with *Brave New World* in 2000, *Dance of Death* in 2003, and *A Matter of Life and Death* in 2006. In 2010, Iron Maiden released *The Final Frontier*, and it was "El Dorado" off of this album that won them their first Grammy Award for Best Metal Performance. In 2015, they released the album *The Book of Souls*. As of 2018, the band shows no signs of stopping. Throughout their

MAKING METAL OUT OF LITERATURE

Iron Maiden is one of the most well-read bands in music. When they need inspiration for a song, they use literary works, which takes their music to a deeper level. Some of their songs and inspirations include:

- "The Trooper": inspired by the poem "Charge of the Light Brigade" by Alfred, Lord Tennyson, which was inspired by the Crimean War

- "To Tame a Land": inspired by the science fiction novel *Dune* by Frank Herbert

- "Sign of the Cross": inspired by Umberto Eco's *The Name of the Rose*

- "Brave New World": inspired by Aldous Huxley's dystopian, sinister novel of the same name that takes place in an "ideal" society

- *Seventh Son of a Seventh Son* album: inspired by Orson Scott Card's *Seventh Son* book, the first in *The Tales of Alvin Maker* series—Alvin Maker is the seventh son of a seventh son

- "The Phantom of the Opera": inspired by the Gaston Leroux book of the same name, the Iron Maiden song tells the story from three points of view—the first verse is from the viewpoint of the Phantom, the second is Christine's, and the third is Raoul's

- "Where Eagles Dare": inspired by the book of the same name by Alistair MacLean, which tells the story of commandos in World War II who try to rescue a general who is a prisoner of war

career, they have sold more than 90 million albums and performed live more than 2,000 times in 63 countries.

Saxon

Saxon was formed when two bands combined in the mid- to late-1970s. Just like other metal bands, they had a hard time getting a recording contract at first. Eventually, they were signed to Carrere Records, and their first, self-titled album was released in 1979. They gained a following in Britain by touring with artists such as Motörhead. They built on this momentum with their follow-up album, *Wheels of Steel*, in 1980. This album had a heavier sound and featured hits such as "Wheels of Steel," "Motorcycle Man," and "747 (Strangers in the Night)." The album hit the top 5 in the United Kingdom (UK), but they were still not popular in the United States. They followed this album with

Saxon struggled to be signed to a record label and then struggled to make it in the United States. However, even as recently as 2018, the band is still recording music and touring.

another release in 1980, called *Strong Arm of the Law*, and 1981's *Denim and Leather*. Four albums and two years into their career, they had yet to gain fame the United States. This became their goal in 1982.

In 1982, Saxon visited the United States on a 38-date tour. They had finally become popular in the United States, and their third UK album, *Strong Arm of the Law*, became their first release in the United States. They then released a live album appropriately titled *The Eagle Has Landed*. Following this in 1983, they released *The Power and the Glory* and separated with Carrere Records, signing with EMI instead. In 1984, they released *Crusader*, which was followed by *Innocence Is No Excuse* in 1985. However, after this album, the band started to slump, in part because of band members leaving and also because of the album *Destiny*, which was not as well-received by fans. In 1992, Saxon got back to their British metal roots with *Forever Free*, followed by *Dogs of War* in 1995, *Unleash the Beast* in 1997, *Metalhead* in 1999, and *Killing Ground* in 2001. Around this time, they also embarked on their first tour in the United States in a decade. Although their popularity waned in America, the band continued to connect with their longtime fans, releasing new music and touring. In 2018, they released their 22nd album, *Thunderbolt*.

Diamond Head

Diamond Head came out of the NWOBHM, and they seemed destined for success with their debut album. They even received recognition from Metallica. However, the band experienced a series of breakups, and fame has still largely escaped them. Diamond Head's most acclaimed album is their debut album, *Lightning to the Nations*. This album was a landmark album in the NWOBHM era and also later influenced bands such as Megadeth and Metallica. Their third studio album, *Canterbury*, was more rock than metal. The band toured with Black Sabbath in 1983 to promote their album, but

around this time, their record label suggested changing management. The band resisted, was dropped from the label, and began working on an album that they financed themselves. However, their manager failed to get them a record deal, and a lack of financing forced the band to break up in 1985, just five years after the release of their debut album.

It was not until 1991 that the band reunited with some of the original members as well as new members. Their fourth album, *Death and Progress*, was released in 1993 and included guests Dave Mustaine of Megadeth and Tony Iommi. The band also picked up new fans after Metallica released an album of cover songs, *Garage Inc.*, which included four songs by Diamond Head.

In 2004, Diamond Head released their fifth album, *All Will Be Revealed*, which was followed by a tour with Megadeth in 2005. This same year was the 25th anniversary of the NWOBHM, and Diamond Head headlined an anniversary show. This show gave the band its first DVD and a live album called *It's Electric*.

In 2007, their sixth album, *What's In Your Head?*, was released, but it was not until 2015 that their seventh, self-titled album was released. Throughout the years, Diamond Head has remained a popular band among fans, and although not as critically acclaimed, they have left their imprint on metal fans and other bands who have used their music for inspiration for their own work.

Def Leppard

Another NWOBHM band that survived the peak of the genre is Def Leppard. They are one of the most recognizable bands in music history and have a large collection of anthems (songs that speak to a mass group of people). They formed in the late 1970s and released an extended play (EP) album on their own label, which ushered in the NWOBHM period. This was followed by their first official release in 1980 with Mercury records, called *On Through the Night*. The album hit number 15 in the UK and 51 on the Billboard record charts. Def Leppard is a unique band with a legacy, and this started right with their first release—they immediately started touring, even in the United States. This was unusual because it generally takes several years for a band to be recognized in a country other than their own. In 1981, they released *High 'n' Dry*, which had anthems such as "High 'n' Dry (Saturday Night)" and "Bringin' On the Heartbreak." Def Leppard continued to release hit albums throughout the years, including an album

released in 2015. However, while their early releases ushered in the NWOBHM period, Def Leppard's music later shifted toward rock.

Mötley Crüe

In the early 1980s, a hair metal band emerged that influenced music for more than 30 years. Hair metal is a term often used interchangeably with pop metal—it featured glam rock fashion from the 1970s, guitar riffs, and pop-influenced hooks in the songs. The most celebrated band to come out of this era and find long-lasting success is Mötley Crüe, which switched from hair metal to rock in later years. Each band member became an icon, and the band as a whole is as iconic for their antics as they are for their music.

Mötley Crüe formed in 1981 with bassist Nikki Sixx, guitarist Mick Mars, drummer Tommy Lee, and singer Vince Neil. In November of the same year, their first album, *Too Fast for Love*, was released and included the hit song of the same name. In 1983, their follow-up album, *Shout at the Devil*, was released and featured the hit "Shout at the Devil" and a cover of the Beatles' "Helter Skelter." As Konow wrote,

The songs on the Shout at the Devil *album were a perfect reflection of the band's attitude—*

*Mötley Crüe, consisting of Nikki Sixx (left), Mick Mars (right), Tommy Lee
(center back), and Vince Neil (center front), had a three-decade career in music.*

angry, mean, and aggressive. Mick Mars's guitar sound was thick as fog with distortion … Tommy Lee completed his drum tracks with the enthusiasm of a child unwrapping his presents at Christmas. He had the timing of a metronome and would throw his entire body into every hit. Nikki Sixx was a mediocre bass player, and it would take him four to five hours to record the bass line of each song.[23]

The album sold 100,000 copies per week right when it was released and would go on to sell more than 3 million copies. For their third album, called *Theatre of Pain*, Mötley Crüe did another cover, this time of Brownsville Station's "Smokin' in the Boys Room." This song and the ballad "Home Sweet Home" drove the album sales, and *Theatre of Pain* sold more than 2 million copies. Following albums continued the band's streak of success, with *Girls, Girls, Girls* selling 2 million copies and *Dr. Feelgood* selling 4 million.

The band adopted an infamous rock and roll lifestyle. Nikki Sixx would cover his pants in rubbing alcohol and set them on fire onstage. Offstage, he developed a heroin addiction that he later wrote about in his book, *The Heroin Diaries*. Meanwhile, Neil was convicted of vehicular manslaughter in 1985,

when he killed Nicholas "Razzle" Dingley of the band Hanoi Rocks in a high-speed drunk driving accident. Neil hit an oncoming car, and the driver ended up in a coma for a month and suffered permanent brain damage. Neil spent less than a month in jail, did 200 hours of community service, and paid $2.6 million to the victims' families. After Neil's verdict for the accident, drunk-driving laws became tougher in Los Angeles, California, where the accident occurred.

In 1992, Neil was fired and replaced with John Corabi, who was then fired two years later, allowing Neil to reunite with his former bandmates. In 1997, the band released *Generation Swine*, which had songs that explored industrial metal, but the album was poorly received. This album was followed by *New Tattoo* in 2000 and *Saints of Los Angeles* in 2008. In between these two releases, the band wrote *The Dirt: Confessions of the World's Most Notorious Rock Band*. Even though they took hiatuses of a few years in between albums, they did not actually leave the public eye and were involved in reality TV shows or other bands. In addition to *The Heroin Diaries*, Nikki Sixx wrote *This Is Gonna Hurt: Music, Photography, and Life Through the Distorted Lens of Nikki Sixx* and started a new rock band, Sixx:A.M. In 2015, Mötley Crüe retired from touring, and in 2018, a film version of *The Dirt* was produced. The movie stars former *Game of Thrones* actor Iwan Rheon as Mick Mars, Daniel Webber as Vince Neil, Douglas Booth as Nikki Sixx, and Machine Gun Kelly as Tommy Lee.

Emerging Subgenres

The NWOBHM period may have been short, but some bands, such as Iron Maiden and Def Leppard, came out of that era and found lasting fame worldwide, either in the metal genre or in the rock genre. As the 1980s progressed, new bands that were influenced by the first metal heavyweights such Black Sabbath emerged. These bands, including Metallica and Anthrax, set the stage for new kinds of metal, and subgenres started to emerge along with a new complexity from classical influences.

CHAPTER THREE

The Big *Four*

While the NWOBHM era was short-lived, it greatly influenced a development of louder, harder, and faster metal known as thrash metal. However, the tempo, or rate of speed of a song, is not enough to classify thrash metal. As Deena Weinstein wrote in *Heavy Metal: The Music and its Culture*, "Speed/thrash [metal] was most directly influenced by NWOBHM groups, such as Venom, Diamond Head, and Iron Maiden, all of which made rhythmic innovations ... The speed/thrash subgenre can be understood to represent as much a transformation of attitude as a change in music."[24]

The lyrical content of thrash bands also broke off from typical metal lyrics. As Weinstein wrote,

Lyrics focus on the bleak but concrete horrors of the real or possibly real world: the isolation and alienation of individuals, the corruption of those in power, and the horrors done by people to one another and the environment.

As the code of the speed/thrash subculture crystalized, groups took names that embodied it. Anthrax, Nuclear Assault, Slayer, Megadeth, Flotsam and Jetsam, Vio-lence, Sacred Reich, Suicidal Tendencies, Annihilator, and Sepultura.[25]

Thrash music was initially seen as an underground phenomenon, with bands being signed to independent, or "indie," labels instead of major labels. The scene erupted between the years of 1981 and 1983 in California, especially in Los Angeles and San Francisco. By 1982, the thrash scene emerged, with fans sharing the bands' demo tapes. The fan base, therefore, grew rapidly for these bands.

Big Four Controversy

From this thrash metal scene emerged four bands who would define the genre. The Big Four is widely accepted as consisting of

Megadeth, Slayer, Anthrax, and Metallica. However, determining who the Big Four should be is a topic of controversy among metal fans. Some people think it should be the "Big Six" and include Exodus and Testament. Others think that one of the Big Four bands should be removed, such as Slayer, and replaced with a band such as Exodus. Even members of the thrash metal scene have their own ideas on the Big Four. Steve "Zetro" Souza of Exodus believes the Big Four should actually be called the Big One (meaning Metallica) and the Other Three (meaning Anthrax, Slayer, and Megadeth) because, as Souza said, "Metallica sits on their own."[26]

Souza also explained why he

Exodus invented certain ways of drumming and picking the guitar that made an impact on metal music. However, they are not formally considered one of the Big Four—although some people believe they should be.

does not believe his band should be included in the Big Four:

Personally, I don't pay attention to that necessarily ... I was in the Bay Area in the beginning, before I was even a member of EXODUS, so I remember who was the forefathers of thrash. I mean, Tom [Hunting, EXODUS drummer] invented that drum beat. That [guitar] picking style was from Gary [Holt, EXODUS guitarist]—that's where the genesis of that came from.[27]

Even though Exodus band members invented certain styles that were influential in the creation of thrash metal, therefore making them incredibly influential, what the Big Four comes down to is money and popularity. As Souza explained,

I think what [the media] did [when they came up with the 'Big Four'] was they took the four bands who were probably the most successful in the initial period of thrash metal—from, say, '85 or '84 to '90. If you were to go off popularity, if you were gonna go off record sales, you would have to say ANTHRAX, Megadeth, METALLICA and SLAYER.[28]

Metallica

Metallica formed in 1981 with the original lineup of James Hetfield, Lars Ulrich, Dave Mustaine, and Ron McGovney. In 1982, the band performed their first show together, which consisted largely of NWOBHM cover songs. Their first demo tape, *No Life 'Til Leather*, was released a few months later. The band quickly became famous before they even released their official debut album because of fans trading their demo tapes. However, a year after the band formed, they had their first personnel change when McGovney left the band in December 1982 and Cliff Burton officially joined a few months later, in February 1983.

Meanwhile, the husband-and-wife team of Jon and Marsha Zazula were running Rock 'N' Roll Heaven, their own record store in New Jersey. They would frequently play metal bands' demo albums in the store, including Metallica's *No Life 'Til Leather*, which grabbed the attention of shoppers who came into the store. Around this same time, Metallica finally got an album deal with Megaforce Records, the Zazulas' indie record label in New York City. The band headed to the East Coast to record their debut album, and while they were there, they also made copies of their demo with Jon Zazula for him to sell at the store. The tapes sold quickly and in large numbers, thus growing Metallica's fan base even more.

Metallica formed in 1981 and quickly gained fans because the fans would trade the band's demo tapes.

However, in April 1983, the band had another personnel change. Mustaine was told he was no longer in the band, and they replaced him with Kirk Hammett, who is still in Metallica as of 2018. A month after being added to the band, Hammett began recording *Kill 'Em All* with the rest of Metallica in Rochester, New York. The album was released on July 25, 1983, and around this time, Metallica released a series of hits that were instant classics, including "Seek and Destroy" and "The Four Horsemen." The album was well-received and allowed them to immediately start on their second studio album, *Ride the Lightning*, which included hits such as "For Whom the Bell Tolls" and "Fade to Black." "Fade to Black" was a song about suicide, which was attacked by people who were anti-metal and believed the song was pro-suicide. However, this belief was false, and the band actually received many letters from fans who told them the song saved their lives.

Around this time, Metallica's lyrics also became more political. As Konow wrote,

Once Hetfield and Ulrich could afford a TV set, they watched the news religiously; later they called the years they wrote these songs "the CNN years." The song "Ride the Lightning" was about capital punishment and someone innocent being executed by mistake. "For Whom the Bell Tolls" was about the atrocities of war; the massive, chiming bell at the beginning of the song is reputed to be a doorbell.[29]

Ride the Lightning was also the last album with the Megaforce label. In 1984, the band signed up with major label Elektra Records, which re-released *Ride the Lightning*. The following year, Metallica was back in the studio to work on their third album, which became one of their most acclaimed: *Master of Puppets*.

Highs and Lows

The year 1986 held promise for Metallica. In March, they released *Master of Puppets*, which gained them even more fans and reached the top 30 of the album charts—even without MTV or frequent radio airplay. The band had many things going for them; their fans loved them, and they were making music on their own terms. As Byron Hontas, a publicist who worked on both *Ride the Lightning* and *Master of Puppets*, said, "Metallica knew where they wanted to go … they had their own direction musically. They didn't want to do makeup; black was their thing. Their music was extremely aggressive, and people didn't know how to take it."[30] Additionally, they were down-to-earth—they did not give the impression that they thought they were too good for their fans. This gained them a level of respect from their fans that future bands learned from. As Konow stated,

The fans felt a close bond with Metallica and were possessive of them. They weren't larger-than-life icons whom you needed ten backstage passes to get close to. The fans looked onstage and saw themselves. Metallica wore basic T-shirts and jeans on stage, and had no "image" to speak of. They made their music the No. 1 focus instead of doing their hair.[31]

In addition, in these early years of the band's history, meeting the band was something that was actually common. During their *Ride the Lightning* and *Master of Puppets* shows, the band stayed late after shows to do meet and greets with their fans. This stemmed from Hetfield remembering the feeling of staying late after concerts when he was younger, hoping to meet the musicians, only to have the musicians ignore the waiting fans and leave in their limousines. Metallica knew that by ignoring their fans, they would lose them.

With this close connection with their fans, the acclaim for their third album, and an opening gig for Ozzy Osbourne, the band seemed to be unstoppable. However, on September 27, 1986, tragedy struck. While the band was on tour in Sweden, their bus skidded on the highway and went off the road. Cliff Burton was thrown out of the bus window from his bunk, where he was sleeping, and when the bus flipped on its side, Burton was pinned underneath it and died. This tragedy shook the band, fans, and the metal scene as a whole. As stated on Metallica's website, "His influence on the musical growth of the band had been enormous, combining the DIY philosophies of jamming and experimenting with an acute knowledge of musical theory."[32] Instead of cancelling their upcoming shows, the band found a short-term replacement for Burton and then a more permanent replacement with Jason Newsted.

Metallica's fourth album, *...And Justice For All*, was released in 1988 and was a turning point for the band. With this album, they released their first music video—for "One"—and were nominated for their first Grammy Award in 1989 for Best Hard Rock/Metal Performance. It was the first time an award like this was offered. Many people thought they knew who would be winning it—Metallica. However, the audience burst out laughing when Alice Cooper opened the envelope and read the winner's name listed inside: Jethro Tull, a flute-fronted folk rock band that has never been considered metal. Cooper had to assure the audience he was not joking, and then the laughter turned to outrage, especially from the band's fans. This incident clearly showed that the recording industry was out of touch. However, in 1990, Metallica won their first Grammy Award for their song "One" and another Grammy in 1991 for a cover of Queen's "Stone Cold Crazy." Even though Metallica has won eight Grammy Awards as of 2018, the 1989 Grammy Awards remain infamous.

"Enter Sandman"

After all of this controversy and outrage over the 1989 Grammy Awards, Metallica experienced worldwide, explosive success due to an album and signature song that are famous among fans. In 1991, Metallica's self-titled album was released, an album that is commonly known as "The Black Album" and contains their signature song, "Enter Sandman." With this album, Metallica employed a new producer, Bob Rock, and he focused Metallica on producing a fuller sound. With his help, the album shot to number 1 around the world and sold more than 16 million copies. Several hit singles were released from the album, including "Nothing Else Matters." Additionally, the band embarked on a 300-show tour that lasted three years, pushing the band's limits.

Their next album, *Load*, was released in 1996, followed by *Reload* in 1997. The band also put out some cover albums during this time. In 2000, another personnel change occurred when Newsted parted ways with Metallica. In 2003, the band released *St. Anger*, followed by a tour with their new bassist Robert Trujillo, who is still in the band as of 2018. Around this time, the band was being documented on film by Joe Berlinger and Bruce Sinofsky. Their film, *Some Kind of Monster*, was released in 2004. However, at the same time, the band had come across a problem—they has been working nonstop for more than two years and needed a break. After a two-year hiatus, they started recording their new album, *Death Magnetic*, which was released in 2008. The album was well-received and charted at number 1. The next year, they were inducted into the Rock and Roll Hall of Fame. In 2010, the Big Four came together for their first joint show in June in Warsaw, Poland. For those who could not be there, a later show was recorded and released on DVD and Blu-Ray with the title, *The Big 4: Live From Sofia, Bulgaria*.

In 2011, Metallica released the album *Lulu*, which was not as well-received as previous albums. However, in true Metallica fashion, they did what they wanted to do for the album. Their next studio album, *Hardwired...to Self-Destruct* was released in 2016. This album was

Metallica has been making music for nearly four decades. As of 2018, they are still touring and making hit albums.

much better received and was the third best-selling album of 2016—Beyoncé and Drake claimed the first two spots. Following this wildly successful album, the band embarked on more tours, including one with Avenged Sevenfold. Nearly four decades after the band formed, they show no signs of slowing down and continue to put out quality music that is made on their own terms, solidifying their position as one of the Big Four of thrash metal and one of the most successful metal acts.

Slayer

One of the most distinctive thrash bands is Slayer. However, they are also one of the most controversial. The band is known for their graphic lyrics that deal with war, death, and more. In addition, "[t]heir full-throttle velocity, wildly chaotic guitar solos, and powerful musical chops painted an effectively chilling sonic background for their obsessive chronicling of the dark side."[33] Slayer began in the early 1980s as a cover band, but then realized using dark imagery in their music would get them both fans and attention. Following this, they wrote the song "Aggressive Protector" for the album *Metal Massacre III*, put out by Metal Blade Records. Shortly after this compilation, Metal Blade Records put out Slayer's album, *Show No Mercy*. In 1985, the band's next album, Hell Awaits, gained them a large fan following. It was still not enough to gain them a national following, however—but that is when Rick Rubin stepped in.

Rick Rubin is a cofounder of Def Jam, and Slayer was signed to this label in 1986. The band immediately generated controversy with their first album for Def Jam. *Reign in Blood* is the first Slayer album with a clear sound, which Rubin contributed to. However, Columbia Records, which distributed the records for Def Jam, did not want to distribute this particular album because of the graphic nature of the lyrics. This controversy actually created a large amount of publicity for the band, though, so another label, Geffen Records, agreed to distribute the album. It was the first Slayer album to chart; it landed low at number 94, but it became an instant classic with fans. As Steve Huey wrote on the AllMusic website,

Combining Slayer's trademark speed metal with the tempos and song lengths (if not structures) of hardcore, along with the band's most disturbing lyrics yet, Reign in Blood *was an instant classic, breaking the band through to a wider audience, and was hailed by some as the greatest speed metal album of all time (some give the nod to Metallica's* Master of Puppets*).*[34]

Reign in Blood was followed by *South of Heaven* in 1988, which disappointed some of the band's followers because it was not as hard as their previous work was. Their following album, *Seasons in the Abyss*, was released in 1990 and found a balance between a commercial sound and the intensity of their previous material. The title track off this album especially became a fan favorite, and with a boost from being featured on the MTV metal show *Headbangers Ball*, the band found themselves at the forefront of the thrash movement alongside Metallica. Aside from the live album *Decade of Aggression*, which was released in 1991 to celebrate 10 years as a band, Slayer remained relatively quiet until 1994.

METAL MUSIC: A HISTORY FOR HEADBANGERS

Upon signing with Def Jam records, Slayer started generating controversy with their albums. They have been highly influential in the death metal subgenre.

In 1994, Slayer's most successful album, *Divine Intervention*, was released. *Divine Intervention* made the top 10 of Billboard's album charts, landing at number 8. After releasing an album of covers and one new song in 1996, Slayer released *Diabolus in Musica* in 1998. In 2001, they released *God Hates Us All*, followed by *Christ Illusion* in 2006 and *World Painted Blood* in 2009. *World Painted Blood* was reminiscent of *Seasons in the Abyss*. In 2013, cofounder and guitarist Jeff Hanneman died of liver failure, but the rest of the band did not let that stop them. Their 12th album, *Repentless*, was released in 2015, with Exodus member Gary Holt replacing Hanneman. In 2018, the band announced they were retiring after a final tour with worldwide dates.

The band was not nominated for

HISTORY LESSONS IN METAL

Metal music has been largely written off by a number of people. Anti-metal people have viewed the genre as Satanic, simple, and influencing people to perform violent acts. Metal fans know these accusations are not true for the majority—some bands do have Satanic music and believe in what they say, but many others do not. The genre is hardly simple, and Judas Priest, Slayer, and other metal bands do not force their fans to perform violent acts—it is the choice of the person committing the act, and the blame for the act cannot be passed from the person who committed it to a song or album.

Proving that metal music is not simplistic but does have dark themes, some metal songs even offer history lessons. Slayer's song "Angel of Death" from *Reign in Blood* is about Josef Mengele, who performed horrific medical experiments on Jewish prisoners at Auschwitz during the Holocaust. The song describes some of the tortures he performed on the prisoners.

In Anthrax's "Indians" from *Among the Living*, they describe more horrors—this time, ones that were committed against the Native Americans by the European colonists. In addition, they express the desire for a prejudice-free world and the message that while the past cannot be taken back, people should learn from these mistakes so they are not repeated in the future.

a Grammy Award until 2001—for the song "Disciple"—and did not win a Grammy until 2006—for the song "Eyes of the Insane." Out of five Grammy nominations, they won two awards. However, the Grammy Awards have been frequently criticized for awarding the nominations and wins to the wrong bands and for being out of touch when it comes to the metal genre, as the 1989 Jethro Tull incident illustrates. As Kim Kelly wrote on Vice, "When it comes to heavy metal and hard rock, the Grammys have always been absolutely excellent at Not Getting It. Metal fans don't expect them to understand why their picks are always so unspeakably lame—if not downright offensive—and what's more, we don't really care that much."[35] Kerry King, guitarist for Slayer, thought it was important when the band won, but he viewed the metal Grammy Award category as ridiculous because of how out of touch the awards show is.

Slayer's importance is acknowledged by fans as well as bands influenced by them. Alex Webster, bassist for Cannibal Corpse, said,

The other thrash bands were good, but they didn't have that dark

sound that SLAYER had. I think that the dark sound that SLAYER had is why they're such an influence on the death metal scene. Because that, to me, is one of the big things, far beyond the vocal stuff, that makes death metal different from regular thrash is the effort to make it sound dark.[36]

Anthrax

Anthrax was formed in 1981, and as of 2018, they are still touring and making music. However, within that career span, they have had a number of changes in the members of the band, including vocalist Joey Belladonna entering and leaving the band on three separate occasions. As of 2018, the band lineup consists of Belladonna, Jonathan Donais, Frankie Bello, Charlie Benante, and Scott Ian. Ian is one of the founding members of the band and has been at the helm of their songwriting throughout their career.

Ian was inspired by the

Anthrax has made an incredible impact on metal music, even through multiple personnel changes.

STEPHEN KING: HORROR AUTHOR AND METAL FAN

Stephen King is one of the most beloved authors in the literary world. He is also one of the most productive authors—he has written more than 59 novels and 200 short stories. Many of his stories have been made into movies, with no signs of the film adaptations stopping. Some of the stories adapted into movies include *It*, *Pet Sematary*, *The Shining*, *The Tommyknockers*, *The Green Mile*, *Christine*, *Desperation*, *Misery*, *Cujo*, and *Firestarter*. What some people may not know is that King is a fan of metal, especially Metallica, Slayer, Judas Priest, and Anthrax. Metal bands also play a role in Stephen King's novels—Judas Priest is featured in *It*, while Anthrax and Megadeth play a role in *The Dark Tower* series.

Additionally, Scott Ian of Anthrax is a huge Stephen King fan. The Anthrax songs "A Skeleton in the Closet" and "Among the Living" were based on Stephen King's *The Stand* and the short story "Apt Pupil" in King's *Different Seasons* collection. "Misery Loves Company" was based on King's *Misery*, and "Lone Justice" was inspired by the first book in *The Dark Tower* series, *The Gunslinger*. The Anthrax song "Antisocial" was even used in the 2017 remake of *It*. However, Anthrax is not the only band to turn to King's horror stories for inspiration. Metallica was inspired by a passage in *The Stand*, taking the album and song title of *Ride the Lightning* from something a character says. The band Blind Guardian has a song called "Tommyknockers" based off the King novel of the same name, and another band called Nightwish based "7 Days to the Wolves" off the fifth book in *The Dark Tower* series, *The Wolves of the Calla*.

NWOBHM movement and wanted to start a band with that type of sound. He is the only original band member to stay with the band throughout their entire career—many musicians passed through various positions in the band in just the first couple years of their formation, and a steady lineup was not achieved until after their debut album, *Fistful of Metal*, was released.

At the beginning of their career, the members of Anthrax began hanging around the Zazulas' store, Rock 'N' Roll Heaven, and were introduced to Metallica's music. Ian had not heard faster music than what Metallica was putting out, which influenced him to pursue things with Anthrax. He said,

It was totally cool hearing that there was this band out in San Francisco that was kind of on the same wavelength of what we were doing … Anthrax were doing our own thing, but it just never seemed like it was gonna work, because we didn't sound like any other band or anything that was

Stephen King is one of the most successful authors in the literary world, especially in the horror genre. He is a fan of metal music, and there are many metal songs based on his work, especially by Anthrax.

around in New York. And then all of a sudden, there's a band out of San Francisco that had their own thing too. It made me feel like maybe there's something going on here.[37]

The Zazulas eventually signed Anthrax to Megaforce Records, although by the time their third album was recorded in 1985, they were with Island Records. Around this time, they had developed a large fan following, due to classic albums such as 1985's *Spreading the Disease* and

the album *Among the Living*, which hinted at the band's social consciousness with songs such as "One World" and "Indians," a song about the brutal treatment of the Native Americans by European colonists. In 1990, the album was certified gold by the RIAA. The band also started experimenting with a rap and metal combination that would become common years later on the 1987 album *I'm the Man*. However, around this time, the band experienced more personnel changes, with Belladonna leaving the band

and John Bush replacing him. Their following albums, *Stomp 442, Volume 8: The Threat Is Real*, and *We've Come for You All*, did not match the earlier success of albums such as *State of Euphoria and Persistence of Time*.

After 2003's *We've Come for You All*, it was eight years until Anthrax released another album, 2011's *Worship Music*. In between these albums, Ian hosted VH1's metal show, *Rock Show*, and frequently contributed as a commentator on other VH1 documentary shows, such as *I Love the '70s, I Love the '80s*, and *I Love the '90s*. He even made an appearance as a walker, or zombie, on the TV show *The Walking Dead* in 2015.

Worship Music was a huge success as a comeback album and was followed by *For All Kings* in 2016. In 2018, the band supported Slayer on the final worldwide tour and released a live DVD, *Kings Among Scotland*, which was filmed at a 2017 show in Glasgow, Scotland. No matter how much the band's lineup changed throughout their career, they have never stopped making a huge impact on metal music.

Megadeth

Megadeth was formed in 1983 by Dave Mustaine and Dave Ellefson after Mustaine was kicked out of Metallica. Mustaine's and Ellefson's goal was to create unique, jazz-oriented metal music that was based on skill and aggression. Mustaine's group set themselves apart from Metallica by adding extra emphasis on their instrumental skills and making the tempo slightly faster, thus making the instruments harsher. This approach worked—Megadeth's first album, *Killing Is My Business...and Business Is Good*, received positive reviews from critics who normally did not deliver good reviews for metal music. This approach to metal also made Megadeth one of the leading bands of the thrash movement. Their concerts were sold out, and each of their albums was certified gold by the RIAA.

In the 1990s, the band toned down their sound. However, that did not reduce the amount of followers they had. In fact, their following increased, and they made it into the top 10 on the charts. Just like Anthrax, Megadeth had many personnel changes throughout their career, and only one band member that stuck around throughout it all—Mustaine. Ellefson was with the band for much of their history, but not from 2004 to 2010. After Metallica found mainstream success in the early 1990s, Megadeth followed, stripping down their sound and being rewarded for it when *Countdown to Extinction* entered the charts at number 2 and went double platinum. This album

Megadeth was formed after Dave Mustaine (shown here) was kicked out of Metallica and went on to become one of the biggest bands in metal.

is considered the band's biggest hit. Seeing the success of this album, Megadeth went back into the studio, releasing *Youthanasia* in 1994. This album again proved to be successful, entering the charts at number 4. *Cryptic Writings*, released in 1997, helped the band become accepted by rock radio. They released *Risk* the following year, which was titled after comments that Lars Ulrich of Metallica made in regard to Megadeth needing to take more risks with their music. In 2001, Megadeth released *The World Needs a Hero*. This album was followed by a break due to a nerve condition in Mustaine's arm, which left him unable to play guitar.

After three years out of the spotlight, the band released their comeback album, *The System Has Failed*, which was followed by *United Abominations* in 2007, *Endgame* in 2009, and *Th1rt3en* in 2011. *Th1rt3en* was the album that signaled Ellefson's return to the band as well as the return of the band's heavier and darker material. In 2013, the band released their 14th studio album, *Super Collider*, followed by *Dystopia* in 2016. The album went straight to number 3 on the Billboard 200 and number 1 on Billboard's Top Rock and Hard Rock Albums chart.

A Brief Fallout

Metallica, Slayer, Anthrax, and Megadeth were all hugely influential in metal music. During this time, these bands greatly advanced the genre, and their music started to be accepted by critics while still being appreciated by fans. However, after the emergence of the Big Four, metal encountered a great deal of controversy, including censorship issues and what has been called the Satanic panic. In addition, thanks to grunge music, metal fell out of favor—but not permanently.

CHAPTER FOUR

Endless
Controversy

In the 1980s, metal started to come under a lot of criticism. However, many other music genres did, too. In fact, even the role-playing game *Dungeons & Dragons* was the target of disapproval. The reasoning behind this is what has grown to be called the Satanic panic. Anything that had hints of the occult, paganism, or anything fantasy-oriented, such as *Dungeons & Dragons*, was viewed as dangerous. All of this was egged on by the Parents Music Resource Center (PMRC), which set out to have a rating system for music.

Satanic panic was not metal's downfall, but after it died down, a new genre stole the spotlight. When bands such as Nirvana became popular during the economic recession of the early 1990s, the angst and despair of this time came across in grunge music, and this music was what became massively popular among teenagers. Even though metal was less popular than it had been, some acts emerged during this time that would still be major influencers in the 2010s.

Pantera

Pantera formed in the early 1980s as Gemini, then changed their name to Eternity before settling on Pantera. They were heavily influenced by bands such as Judas Priest, AC/DC, and KISS, picking up style cues from them. However, when bands such as Metallica and Slayer arrived on the scene, they followed their lead—making what they were doing solely about the music and not about how they were dressed, choosing to perform in clothes that they would wear any other day. While it may not seem like much, as Metallica showed, this small thing makes a band feel more approachable to fans and makes fans feel like they could form their own band someday.

Throughout much of the 1980s, the band released glam metal-inspired music that was largely unsuccessful. However, a major turning point came when the band wanted a heavier sound and vocalist Phil Anselmo was added to the band. The next turning point for Pantera came with the release of their 1990 album *Cowboys From Hell*. This album was their first one with a major record label, and their second, 1992's *Vulgar Display of Power*, put them at the forefront of the metal scene alongside bands such as Metallica, Anthrax, Slayer, and Megadeth. The song "Walk" off of this album is one of their most famous. It has been covered by many bands, both live and on albums; for instance, Disturbed's David Draiman covered it with Breaking Benjamin at a live show in 2016, and Avenged Sevenfold did the same on their DVD-album set *Live in the LBC & Diamonds in the Rough*. Pantera's 1994 album, *Far Beyond Driven*, solidified them as a top metal act, and their song "I'm Broken" received quite a bit of airplay on the radio.

However, at the height of this popularity, the band began to fall apart. In 1996, after the release of *The Great Southern Trendkill*, Anselmo overdosed on heroin. Although he did not die, this took a toll on his health. Additionally, he was working on many side projects that continued to pull him away from Pantera right at the height of their career. The band released a live album in 1997 because it was clear that an actual studio album would not be happening soon. This was followed in 2000 by *Reinventing the Steel*, which ended up being the band's last stu-

dio album. The band went their separate ways after this album, with Anselmo forming the band Down and brothers "Dimebag" Darrell Abbott and Vinnie Paul forming Damageplan.

The official end of Pantera occurred on December 8, 2004, when Dimebag Darrell was murdered during a Damageplan concert. Nathan Gale, the shooter, waited for the band to come on the stage. Once the music started, he jumped a fence and rushed into the club where they were playing, pushing his way past tables, the sound booth, and the bar. Witnesses at the event thought he was going to stage-dive, but instead, he took out a gun and shot Dimebag Darrell. People thought it was part of the band's act until the music stopped and a security guard took down Gale as he kept on shooting into the crowd. He also shot and killed crew member Jeff Thompson, club employee Erin A. Halk, and fan Nathan Bray. Most concertgoers ran away from the scene, but a few ran toward the scene to try to save the victims. One fan, Justin Caudill, tried pulling Dimebag Darrell off the stage. Mindy Reece, a registered nurse, immediately ran to Dimebag Darrell's side, putting pressure on his wounds with a shirt and doing chest compressions for about 20 minutes until paramedics arrived. Once they arrived and checked his condition,

By playing music how they wanted and dressing in everyday clothes, bands such as Pantera (shown here) were more approachable for fans.

he was pronounced dead within minutes. Two other concertgoers, William Wever and Jimmy Van Fossen, did chest compressions and mouth-to-mouth resuscitation on Thompson, who was pronounced dead at the hospital. As Jason Birchmeier wrote on AllMusic,

This much-publicized murder shone the spotlight on Pantera for an extended moment, and amid all of the emotional outpouring and tributes, a consensus arose: in retrospect, there was no greater metal band during the early to mid-'90s than Pantera, who inspired a legion of rabid fans and whose oft-termed "groove metal" style bucked all prevailing trends

ZOMBIES AND HORROR MOVIES

White Zombie was formed in the mid-1980s by Rob Zombie (born Rob Cummings). The band was originally part of the underground scene in New York and grew a following that included Kurt Cobain, but in the early 1990s, they were signed to Geffen Records, who sensed they were about to break out of the underground. Throughout the mid- to late-1980s, they released several records independently, and their first major-label studio album was released in 1992. The release of this album was huge—the music trend at the time was grunge, and White Zombie was heavy metal combined with industrial rock and theatrical elements. This album was propelled by the song "Thunder Kiss '65," which made the

Rob Zombie started the band White Zombie, then went on to have a successful solo career as both a musician and horror film director.

of the day—from hair metal and grunge to nu-metal and rap-metal—and remains singular to this day, as defined by the vocals of Anselmo as it is by the guitar of Dimebag.[38]

In June 2018, fans experienced more sadness with the death of Darrell's brother, Vinnie Paul.

Satanic Panic

Satanic panic took hold in the 1980s, but had its roots many years before then. In the 1960s, Charles Manson led a cult named the Family. He used manipulation techniques to get people—mostly young women—to join it. In 1969, he convinced some members of the Family to commit brutal murders based on his belief that he was destined to start a race war. Between August 9 and 10, pregnant actress Sharon Tate, Abigail Folger, Wojciech Frykowski, Jay Sebring, Steven Parent, and Rosemary and album hit the top 30 within a year. Their follow-up album, *Astro-Creep: 2000— Songs of Love, Destruction and Other Synthetic Delusions of the Electric Head*, was released in 1995 and propelled by another hit, "More Human Than Human." This ended up being their best-selling album, reaching number 6 on the Billboard charts.

Around this time, however, Rob Zombie wanted to start a solo career, which has been much more successful and longer lasting than White Zombie's career. In 1998, Rob Zombie released his debut solo album, *Hellbilly Deluxe*, which went straight to number 5 on the Billboard charts. As of 2018, it has sold more than 3 million copies. The album gave fans exactly what they wanted: It did not stray too far from the much-loved music of White Zombie, and it included computerized sections and heavy guitars that made it appeal to both industrial and metal fans. *Hellbilly Deluxe* was propelled by three singles and fan favorites that are still featured in Rob Zombie's live shows as late as 2018: "Superbeast," "Dragula," and "Living Dead Girl."

In the early 2000s, Rob Zombie began his horror movie directing career with the film *House of 1000 Corpses*, which was followed up with the sequel *The Devil's Rejects* in 2005. In 2018, he filmed the third movie in the series, *3 From Hell*. He has also remade the classic horror film *Halloween* and a sequel to his remake, *Halloween II*.

Leno LaBianca were murdered. All the victims were white, and Manson tried to make it look like the murders had been committed by the Black Panther party in an attempt to pit white and black people against each other. This kind of ritualistic murder ended up sticking in the minds of many.

In 1971, William Peter Blatty released the book *The Exorcist*, which was turned into a film in 1973. It claimed to be based on a true story of demonic possession, and Americans were greatly impacted by this— especially when combined with Manson's cult and ritualistic murders of a few years earlier. In 1969 and 1972, Anton LaVey published books on Satanism, which "reinforced the idea that dark occult rituals had become a routine part of life for many Americans."[39] The Jonestown Massacre of 1978 did not help these ideas and was another example of violence and cult behavior: More than 900 members of a cult led by Jim Jones died when he convinced them to drink poison he had put in a batch of a Kool-Aid-like drink. While many refer to it as mass suicide, others prefer the term mass murder, especially since many people did not want to drink the poison after people started dying around them but were forced to anyway.

Around this time, there was a growing fascination with dark subjects, including the occult and serial killers such as the Zodiac Killer, Ted Bundy, John Wayne Gacy, the Hillside Stranglers, and David Berkowitz. Americans were constantly hearing of cults, the occult, and ritualistic killings, which made them seem like more of a threat than they actually were. Therefore, fear among the public started to rise.

In the 1980s, anxiety and fear increased again due to topics such as the AIDS epidemic, reports of scary killer clowns—a trend that was revived in 2016—and the Tylenol murders of 1982, in which seven people died after taking Tylenol that had been laced with cyanide poison. As fears over death and the occult began to grow, Christianity also experienced growth, with people crusading against the occult. One of these people was "Pat Pulling, who believed her son committed suicide because of an evil Dungeons and Dragons curse." She "crusaded against role-playing games as dangerous and demonic"[40] and was backed by Christian cartoon creator Jack Chick.

Parents Music Resource Center

In 1985, the PMRC, which was led by Tipper Gore, created a list of 15 songs that they determined were inappropriate. Nine of the songs were metal. They wanted music to have ratings and warn listeners and parents if there was any kind of explicit content, including sex, drugs or alcohol, the occult, and violence. Dee Snider of the band Twisted Sister was one of the people who showed up to the Senate hearings to defend music—and angered the court when he had an intelligent defense. However, what was unknown to Snider or anyone else who showed up to defend music was that the PMRC and the Senate had already made a deal with the RIAA. It was not exactly what the PMRC wanted, which was content-specific labeling with an initial for the kind of offensive material one could find on the album, such as "O" for the occult. Instead, it was a general label that can still be found on explicit music today: a black-and-white sticker stating that there is a parental advisory. This actually excited many music buyers; they wanted to purposely buy

Musicians such as Dee Snider (left) showed up at the PMRC's Senate hearings to protest music censorship and labeling. However, the PMRC and U.S. Senate had already made a deal with the RIAA for voluntary album labeling—something that would end up becoming mandatory.

the music they knew people disapproved of as a way to rebel against authority. However, as Snider stated in 2015, musicians' First Amendment right to free speech was eroded; some stores required censored versions of albums to be carried specifically at that store. That meant that the average music buyer was sometimes unaware that the music they were purchasing was not as the artist intended and that content was either completely removed or bleeped out. Instead of the music buyer being able to make a choice as to what version of an album to listen to, it was already decided for them. Since then, the parental advisory sticker that was supposed to be voluntary has become mandatory.

After the PMRC and controversy over censoring music, the media started to join in with documentaries such as *Devil Worship: Exposing Satan's Underground*, which was hosted by Geraldo Rivera in 1988. At this point, metal was dragged even more through the mud and into the ongoing Satanic panic.

Panic Over Metal

In *Devil Worship: Exposing Satan's Underground*, Rivera claimed heavy metal was part of a Satanic conspiracy that was overtaking the United States. Metal was a genre primarily enjoyed by youth at that time, so people believed it was contributing to young people's impressionable minds being overtaken by Satan, or the devil. Metal was not tame music, the way pop was. The sheer difference of it painted it as a villain—something to be blamed for the ills of the nation at that time.

In 1984, a man named Ricky Kasso murdered another man named Gary Lauwers. The murder was brutal and seemed ritualistic, so the media jumped on the opportunity to present Kasso as a Satanist and member of a cult. Additionally, he was wearing an AC/DC shirt when he was arrested, was a metal fan—especially of Black Sabbath and Judas Priest—and therefore, metal

and the crime he committed were linked in the public's minds. In Rivera's documentary, he suggested that there should be a warning label for Satanism, much like there is on cigarettes—although Rivera did not clarify what objects should be labeled. The documentary also suggested that people who listen to metal drink blood and rob graves. The documentary repeatedly linked metal, devil worship, and violent crimes. One 14-year-old who had murdered his mother was a Black Sabbath fan. Ozzy Osbourne was therefore brought into the documentary, talking with Rivera via satellite. Osbourne was asked about the connection between metal and these violent acts but was cut off before he could give a defense of metal. The violent cases the documentary explored did involve some young people who happened to be fascinated with Satan and enjoy metal music. However, what the nearly two-hour documentary ignored was that the music was not responsible for making the person commit the act. Additionally, the people who were mentioned were a sample and by no means represented the entire metal community. For example, years after this documentary aired, people such as Mindy Reece, William Wever, and Jimmy Van Fossen ran into, instead of away from, a dangerous situation to try to save the lives of those who were hurt in the December 2004 shooting at

Dimebag Darrell's show.

Blaming metal music such as Iron Maiden's *The Number of the Beast* was easy—easier than placing the blame on people. The feeling that an average person could be responsible for so much violence created a feeling of unease, and the idea that there was an easy solution—banning metal music—was appealing to many. This attitude stuck throughout the 1990s.

The Controversy of Marilyn Manson

Just as the Satanic panic started to quiet down, Marilyn Manson arrived on the metal scene and generated a great deal of controversy. Manson became infamous early in his career when he ripped apart the Book of Mormon onstage and the founder of the Church of Satan gave him the title of "Reverend." His album *Antichrist Superstar*, released in 1996, resulted in Manson's concerts being protested by civic groups and his music being attacked by the political right and religious groups. However, nothing compared to what happened in 1999.

On April 20, 1999, Eric Harris and Dylan Klebold shot and killed 13 people and wounded more than 20 others before taking their own lives at their high school in Littleton, Colorado. At the time, it was the worst school shooting in the United States. Marilyn Manson was immediately blamed for inspiring Klebold and Harris—even though the two boys did not listen to Manson's music and instead listened to bands that much of America would not have heard of, such as the German metal group Rammstein, although no metal band should have been blamed for the atrocity that Klebold and Harris committed. Marilyn Manson stayed out of the spotlight out of respect for the public after the horrific shooting. In June 1999, he wrote an article in *Rolling Stone* magazine about how responsibility needs to be placed with those who commit the acts. He also opposed publicizing mass murderers' actions and placing their photos on the covers of magazines. Instead, he wrote, murderers should only be punished because giving them publicity creates the idea that it is an acceptable thing to do, when in reality, it is wrong and harmful; what Klebold and Harris did is something that should not be copied for any reason. Manson also reflected on his music as well as history and how blaming an outside factor—such as music or violent video games—and attempting to find messages in music that are not there is wrong. He wrote, "this kind of controversy does not help me sell records or tickets, and I wouldn't want it to. I'm a controversial artist,

MARILYN MANSON

Born Brian Warner, Marilyn Manson started out as a music journalist in the 1980s. While working as a journalist, he started a band and took on his new name—a combination of the names of the late actress Marilyn Monroe and cult leader Charles Manson. The band, originally called Marilyn Manson and the Spooky Kids, became one of the most popular acts in South Florida by playing gigs and self-releasing music. These gigs became especially notable for Manson's makeup, which he still is famous for today, and special effects that he made himself.

In 1993, Manson was offered a contract with Nothing Records—a label started by Trent Reznor of Nine Inch Nails—and was also offered a slot opening for Nine Inch Nails. In 1994, Manson's debut, *Portrait of an American Family*, was released. With this album, Manson grew a larger following, and the next album, *Smells Like Children*, was a success. This album was especially propelled by his cover of "Sweet Dreams (Are Made of This)" by the Eurythmics.

Antichrist Superstar, released in 1996, debuted at number 3 on the album charts. It was the first album in a trilogy that included 1998's *Mechanical Animals* and *Holy Wood (In the Shadow of the Valley of Death)*. *Antichrist Superstar* also spawned Manson's most recognizable song: "The Beautiful People." *Holy Wood* was followed by *The Golden Age of the Grotesque* in 2003. This album was on many critics' top-10 lists at the end of 2003. In 2015, Manson released what is considered one of his best albums—*The Pale Emperor*. For this album, he grew even more as an artist and joined forces with Tyler Bates, who composed scores for films such as *Guardians of the Galaxy*, *Watchmen*, and *300*. This album was Manson's sixth straight top-10 album. He teamed up with Bates again for 2017's *Heaven Upside Down*. Even

one who dares to have an opinion and bothers to create music and videos that challenge people's ideas in a world that is watered-down and hollow."[41]

Buffalo Death Metal

Cannibal Corpse—one of the most successful bands in death metal, and also one of the most important—was formed in 1988 in Buffalo, New York. In 1989, a demo tape allowed the band to get a contract with Metal Blade Records, and the following year, *Eaten Back to Life* was released. This album was followed by others in 1991 and 1992 that helped the band gather quite a following. However, as with many bands in the 1980s and 1990s, they were also the center of a lot of controversy due to their horror style imagery, extreme

Marilyn Manson is one of the most controversial performers in music. His fans still appreciate his music even decades after his shocking career began.

through all the controversy surrounding Marilyn Manson, whether it is his stage show or the topics of his songs, he continues to release chart-topping music that is well-received among those who appreciate his artistry.

sounds, and graphic lyrics. As a result, their albums were banned in some places.

Cannibal Corpse's sound did not change much throughout their career, but fans did not care and continued following their music. Throughout their three-decade career, they have released 14 full-length albums, with the latest being released in 2017. Called *Red and Black*, it exhibits more of an aggressive, raw sound and musicianship than previous recent releases. Even 14 albums and three decades into their career, the band still has the ability to shock and set standards in music.

Opeth

The Swedish band Opeth was formed in 1990 by Mikael Åkerfeldt and Peter Lindgren, and it has become

Opeth has seemingly created their own genre of metal because of the diverse nature of their music.

one of the most important in metal. Their music has taken different turns and shown a diversity that has resulted in Opeth completely creating their own sound and almost creating their own genre. Throughout their career, they have experimented with acoustic instrumentation, soft vocals, and more. The diversity of their music and the fact that an album from them can be death metal or an acoustic set has allowed them to appeal to many different people and inspire other bands. Their earlier, heavier material in particular has been a huge influence. Åkerfeldt was born in the mid-1970s, so he listened to early metal such as that from the NWOBHM. However, Åkerfeldt is merely influenced by this material and invents his own sound instead of copying others. Opeth's unique sound has been evident since their debut album, *Orchid*, which was released in 1995 by Candlelight Records and set the tone for death metal. This was followed in 1996 by *Morningrise*. Around this time, Century Records showed interest in the band and wanted to release their first two albums in the United States as well as a new third album.

In 1998, *My Arms, Your Hearse* was released, which was followed by *Still Life*. By this time, the band was at the forefront of the progressive metal scene, with *Still Life* showing more progressive metal influences than its predecessor. Ten years after the band formed, they played live in the United States for the first time at a metal festival called *Milwaukee Metalfest*.

In 2001, the band gained even more recognition among metal fans with their album *Blackwater Park*, which was listed on *Rolling Stone*'s 100 Greatest Metal Albums list. This growing recognition resulted in the band releasing their next two albums rapidly— *Deliverance* in 2002 and *Damnation* in 2003. The band has always done exactly what they want to when they feel like it. As Åkerfeldt said in a *Rolling Stone* article, "We're still a metal band, when we want to [be] … But of course sometimes we don't want to be the heaviest band. Sometimes we want to be the most quiet band, or the most whatever else."[42] This was proven with *Damnation*, which stripped away any hints of heavy metal and focused on acoustic instrumentation instead. With their next albums, *Ghost Reveries* and *Watershed*, they returned to their metal roots. However, *Watershed* also signaled the end of their death metal sound.

In 2011, they released *Heritage*, which incorporated new influences such as Swedish folk music. This was followed by *Pale Communion* in 2014, which explored sounds from the 1960s, 1970s, and 1980s. In 2016, Opeth released *Sorceress*. Åkerfeldt stated that during the production of this album, his music tastes became even wider, and he started listening to jazz music by artists such as Miles Davis. Åkerfeldt said,

I can only talk from my perspective and taste here, but we offer diversity that's not really present in the scene today. Whatever genre. We've always been a special band. We've gotten a lot of [hassle] for being different. We still do. Our time will come, I think. It comes down to perseverance. It comes down to not giving up or giving in to public opinion. Music is about doing your own thing or going your own way.[43]

Chthonic

Chthonic (pronounced "thonic") was formed in the 1990s in Taiwan and has been referred to as the Black Sabbath of Asia—they are Asia's biggest metal band, although their influence spreads beyond music. Bassist Doris Yeh advocates for a women's rights organization; drummer Dani Wang is involved in music education; keyboard player CJ Kao and guitarist Jesse Liu work on the production of many Taiwanese bands' albums; and front man Freddy Lim was chair of the Taiwan branch of Amnesty International, an organization that fights for human rights, between 2012 and 2016. Lim is a political activist, which is something that comes across in both his music and personal life. In 2016, he was elected legislator for Taipei's Fifth District as part of the New Power Party, which was founded by Lim and other activists from the Sunflower Movement. (The Sunflower Movement was a reaction to the Cross-Strait Service Trade Agreement, which would allow investment opportunities between China and Taiwan. Many people, mostly youth, protested this and hoped Taiwan would remain independent and not be assimilated into China. The agreement was not formally approved.) As a result of these political viewpoints, as of 2018, Chthonic is banned from China. The lyrics of their songs cannot even be looked up in China. In 2003, the band played in the United States, but before they arrived there, they received threatening emails from Chinese students who were studying in the United States.

Chthonic's songs focus on Taiwanese folk stories, mythology, and history, and they also include political stances, which is another part of why the band is not allowed in China. Their music incorporates melodies from Taiwanese operas, traditional Taiwanese folk music, and even traditional instruments such as the *pgaku* flute, *hen*,

*Chthonic invented the genre Orient metal,
and their lyrics focus on history and mythology.*

and *zheng*. Additionally, their music has been placed into a number of genres, including death metal, folk metal, and black metal. The band, however, has chosen their own genre—Orient metal—because it is metal that is specific to Taiwan.

Each of Chthonic's albums tells a complete story. According to the band's website, the stories of their albums are as follows:

Bú-Tik
*Running through violent scenes
across time and space, would
the answer appear at the end?*

Souls Reposed Trilogy
[Seediq Bale]
*Walking through the Valley of
Death onto the Bridge of
Rainbow as Seediq Bale.*

[Mirror of Retribution]
Defending the purest faith with the ultimate sacrifice.
[Takasago Army]
After leading a life on the battleground, he finally sees who he really is as he washed off the bloodstain on his body.

Relentless Recurrence
The seal imposed upon Nataoji had been lifted off, and the ghost has revived.

9th Empyrean
A struggle for power in the world of deities on the mother island.[44]

In 2014, Chthonic released an acoustic album called *Timeless Sentence*. In December 2017, they released a new song, "Souls of the Revolution," which featured Randy Blythe of the band Lamb of God.

Metal Emerges Victorious

Metal survived the spread of the grunge genre in the 1990s, the rising popularity of which largely pushed metal aside, with a few new acts remaining popular past these tough times in the music industry. It also survived the Satanic panic controversy. However, while it survived the 1990s, the genre did not thrive; it remained popular with loyal fans, but did not attract as many new ones as it previously had. Fortunately, this changed in the 2000s, when metal experienced a revival.

CHAPTER FIVE

Metal
Today

Metal has had virtually no mainstream support throughout its history, which makes its continuing popularity impressive. Certain artists, such as Metallica, Ozzy Osbourne, Iron Maiden, and Avenged Sevenfold, have experienced incredible success. However, even with this success, there is little representation at the Grammys. There have been mixed reactions to this; while it has generated controversy, many fans simply do not care because they know what they like and will support it no matter what an awards show says. In addition, metal tends to rebel against the mainstream, focusing on musicianship, and bands as well as fans largely do not care about things such as music awards. Despite its lack of awards, the genre remains relevant; in the 2000s, there have been metal music festivals, such as *Ozzfest* and *Mayhem Festival*, among others that feature a variety of genres, in which fans can see their favorite bands as well as be introduced to new music.

The variety of artists and subgenres available for metal fans to listen to shows that not only is metal diverse, it is growing and thriving.

Nothing Stands In Their Way: Lacuna Coil

Lacuna Coil was formed in the 1990s, and the combination of Cristina Scabbia's and Andrea Ferro's vocals over the hard instrumentation quickly gained recognition among Italy's goth metal scene. This recognition increased as they toured in Europe with bands such as Moonspell. While they released albums such as their self-titled EP, *In a Reverie*, *Half Life*, and *Unleashed Memories*, their album *Comalies* is what allowed the band to break out.

Released in 2002, *Comalies* gathered quick praise in the metal world, especially with singles such as their first one, "Heaven's a Lie," and "Swamped." Attention surrounding the band grew even more as they toured with influential metal bands such as Opeth and played at *Ozzfest* in 2004 and 2006. Also in 2006, the band debuted a harder sound with their album *Karmacode*. *Comalies* was popular among metal fans, but it did not land well on the Billboard album charts, only reaching number 178. However, the recognition the band had been building with that album laid the groundwork for *Karmacode* to really break through—it reached number 28 on the Billboard charts.

After the wild success of *Karmacode*, Lacuna Coil embarked on more tours, especially metal festivals, and released the album *Shallow Life* in 2009. This album was even more successful, peaking at number 16 on the Billboard charts. However, it also divided the fan base because it broke away from their previous heavier sound. Following *Shallow Life*, *Dark Adrenaline*, which went back to a slightly harder sound, was released in 2012 and is their highest ranking album on the Billboard charts to date, reaching spot 15. The album included songs such as "Trip the Darkness," "Kill the Light," and even a cover of R.E.M.'s song "Losing My Religion." In 2014, they released *Broken Crown Halo*, which was significant for many reasons.

Lacuna Coil's fame took off with the release of the albums Comalies *and* Karmacode.

Broken Crown Halo marked the last Lacuna Coil album with longtime band members Cristiano Migliore and Cristiano Mozzati, who both decided to leave the band at the same time. The first single off the album was appropriately called "Nothing Stands In Our Way." The way the band recorded this album was also different. Created in an old recording studio in Milan, Italy, they recorded with vintage gear, resulting in a crushing sound that was praised by critics and fans alike. Two years after *Broken Crown Halo*, *Delirium* was released, and Marco Biazzi left the band. This album is the band's heaviest. Guitars were tuned down, Ferro's and Scabbia's vocals were harsh, and the music also features double bass drums. In 2017, the band announced it would be a few years before another album was released to follow up *Delirium* because they were focusing on celebrating their 20-year anniversary with surprises for fans. In early 2018, they released a limited edition box set of their entire discography, live material, and rare songs. Also in 2018, their book *Nothing Stands In Our Way* was released. The book featured photographs as well as a history of the band. Two decades into Lacuna Coil's career, the band continues to release music that fans love and critics praise.

Atreyu

Atreyu was formed in the 1990s with Alex Varkatzas on vocals, Brandon Saller on drums and vocals, Dan Jacobs and Travis Miguel on guitar, and Chris Thomson on bass. The band emerged during the explosion of rap-metal at the beginning of the 2000s. They released an EP, *Fractures in the Facade of Your Porcelain Beauty*, in 2001, then their first full-length album, *Suicide Notes and Butterfly Kisses*, in 2002. During this rap-metal period, the band established themselves as something different, and fans responded. Their songs combine musicianship with tight instrumental arrangements and solid songwriting. In addition, they have two vocalists, with Varkatzas handling the screamed vocals and Saller being responsible for the melodic singing.

Their musicianship was evident immediately when they debuted. Singles off of *Suicide Notes and Butterfly Kisses* included songs such as "Ain't Love Grand" and "Lip Gloss and Black," which was the second single off the album. This song was responsible for attracting a large amount of attention to the band; it features exhilarating instrumentation that is famous among fans. Also famous is the line "Live, Love, Burn, Die"[45] from the song, which is still a signature line among fans—even nearly two decades after it debuted. Before recording their follow-up album, however, Thomson was replaced by Marc McKnight, who is still with the band as of 2018.

Suicide Notes and Butterfly Kisses was an impressive debut for the band, but their next album, *The Curse*, catapulted them to fame. Released in 2004, the album featured songs such as "The Crimson," "Bleeding Mascara," and "This Flesh a Tomb." To keep their momentum going, the band started rapidly touring in support of their albums as well as to establish themselves in the music business. In 2004 and 2006, they joined the *Ozzfest* lineup, and in between, they were with the *Vans Warped Tour*.

Also in 2006, they released another album, *A Death-Grip on Yesterday*, which was well-received and included songs such as "Ex's and Oh's" and "Shameful." While *The Curse* only reached number 32 on the Billboard charts, *A Death-Grip on Yesterday* went up to number 9. This album was followed up with more touring. In 2008, Atreyu joined another festival, the *Rockstar Taste of Chaos*, which included another heavyweight: Avenged Sevenfold.

Their next album, *Lead Sails Paper Anchor*, was released in 2007. The album was a departure for their band. While it was still well-received, reaching number 8 on the Billboard charts—their highest rank on the charts as of 2018—this album extremely divided their fans. Considering Atreyu's exhilarating previous releases, their fans were highly anticipating this release and expecting the heavier material that they enjoyed. However, while Varkatzas did not completely stop screaming for the whole album, his screaming is mostly absent from the release. This resulted in a disappointing album for some fans, who saw more promise in this album than what was delivered. The band's following album, *Congregation of the Damned*, was viewed by some fans as an improvement over *Lead Sails Paper Anchor*, especially the song "Coffin Nails." However, it was still not what the band had gained a following for. In 2016, Varkatzas explained the vast difference between these two albums and their earlier work. For *Lead Sails Paper Anchor*, they switched to a major record label, Hollywood Records. The band wanted to make the type of music they had previously been doing, but the record company had a different idea for *Lead Sails Paper Anchor*. Then, once the band had released an album that was not as hard as other music they had done, they found it difficult to go to the record label and tell them they wanted their next album to be metal.

After *Congregation of the Damned*, the band went on a hiatus

Atreyu emerged during the explosion of rap-metal during the early 2000s and quickly established themselves as heavyweights of the metalcore genre.

to pursue other music interests—such as Saller's band Hell or Highwater—and focus on their families. Their next album was released in 2015 with a different record label—Spinefarm Records. *Long Live* saw the band return to the much-loved harder music that was featured on albums such as *The Curse*. While many were hesitant to hear what the comeback album would sound like, in the end, they found themselves pleased by the results—and by the fact that the kings of the metalcore genre were back. In 2018, M. Shadows of Avenged Sevenfold let slip that he had heard the new Atreyu album and that it sounded great, which hinted that a new album would be forthcoming.

Slipknot

Slipknot self-released an album in 1996, but their 1999 major label debut was unlike anything else the metal world had encountered,

MENTAL HEALTH AND CREATIVITY

Sometimes people think that using drugs or alcohol or not treating mental health issues such as depression and anxiety allows them to be more creative. They may think it allows them to tap into a mindset they would not be able to access if they were taking medication. Alex Varkatzas of Atreyu acknowledged that he did this for the creation of the *Lead Sails Paper Anchor* album. He stated that he has severe anxiety and that, in the past, antidepressant and anti-anxiety medications helped him perform the duties of his job, such as touring and writing music. However, while writing the songs of *Lead Sails Paper Anchor*, he stopped taking his medication. He said in an interview that he was using music in an attempt to deal with the emotions he was feeling, rather than taking medication or drinking alcohol to deal with them. Turning to alcohol to deal with emotions should not be done as it often causes even more problems, and when a metal health issue has been diagnosed, it should be treated according to a plan worked out with a mental health professional. At the time, Varkatzas admitted that quitting his prescribed medication had a negative effect on his emotional stability, saying, "I lose my mind a couple times a day now."[1] In recent years, uncontrolled mental illness has also contributed to many suicides in music in general, including Chester Bennington of Linkin Park and Chris Cornell of Audioslave and Soundgarden. As author John Green wrote,

> *Mental illness is stigmatized, but it is also romanticized. If you google the phrase "all artists are," the first suggestion is "mad." We hear that genius is next to insanity; we see Carrie Mathison on* Homeland *going off her meds so that she can discover the identity of the terrorists and save America.*

> *Of course, there are kernels of truth here: Many artists and storytellers do live with mental illness. But many don't. And what I want to say today I guess is that you can be sane and be an artist, and also that if you are sick, getting help—although it is hard and exhausting and inexcusably difficult to access—will not make you less of an artist.*[2]

1. Quoted in Chris Harris, "Atreyu Singer Tries to Stay Sane; plus Dark Fortress, Brutal Truth & More News That Rules, in *Metal File*," MTV News, August 23, 2007. www.mtv.com/news/1567801/atreyu-singer-tries-to-stay-sane-plus-dark-fortress-brutal-truth-more-news-that-rules-in-metal-file/.

2. John Green, "My NerdCon Stories Talk About Mental Illness and Creativity," Medium, October 15, 2016. medium.com/@johngreen/my-nerdcon-stories-talk-about-mental-illness-and-creativity-bfac9c29387e.

and this is the theme for the entire band's work. As John Hill wrote on Vice,

Right from their self-titled major label debut in 1999, it was obvious there was something vastly different about Slipknot. You weren't watching some band of dudes shred on stage, you were watching a gang of nine individuals create varieties of sound and noise that would be unlike anything else you'd heard. Slipknot isn't just a band, it's an identity that has inspired millions of fans around the world and united them.[46]

As attention-grabbing as their music is, the masks that each band member wears grab attention just as much. What is even more remarkable about Slipknot is that they were not aiming for the success they achieved. Their self-titled album was released in 1999, and they were added at the last minute to the *Ozzfest* lineup for that same year. In fact, their album had not even come out before they were added to the *Ozzfest* lineup—it was released halfway through the tour. As Slipknot member Corey Taylor said, "We went into this so positive, there were no expectations whatsoever. Because who we were, and what we were as a band, there were actually less expectations. No one expected us to win, least of all us."[47] Taylor added that they could tell something was happening during *Ozzfest* and that they were building quite a following. This was proven when, three days after finishing with *Ozzfest*, they were placed third on the bill of the *Coal Chamber* tour, right before Machine Head. The craze around them built, so halfway through the tour, they were switched to be the direct support band, which means they switched places with Machine Head and became the second to last band to play. This was done because many concertgoers would leave the show right after Slipknot was done playing.

The hype over Slipknot would not die down. Not only was their album great, but their live show also was, and still is, just as good. In fact, in 2016, they were named one of the best metal bands to see live by *LA Weekly*. A lot happens at a Slipknot show, partially because there are nine band members putting all their energy into a show that involves fire as well as percussionists on drum risers that not only lift up, but also spin. Slipknot's name is often mentioned by people who are talking about the best band they have seen live. They put on a highly energetic set—so energetic that Clown (Shawn Crahan) sliced his head open on his drum kit twice on their first *Ozzfest* tour. Even with a head wound, he played right up to the end of their sets. The fans—or maggots, as the band affectionately calls them—have responded to the band's dedication and energy since their first tour. In January 2000, not even a year after their first major-label debut was released, the album was certified gold by the RIAA. In May 2000, the album was certified platinum, and as of 2018, it has been certified two times multiplatinum.

There was much anticipation for the band's follow-up. *Iowa* was released in 2001 and shot to number 3 on the Billboard chart. The album was released in August of that year, and by October, it was certified platinum. However, despite this success, the tragedy of the terrorist attacks in New York City on September 11, 2001, caused certain songs to be temporarily pulled from the radio out of fears that they might be insensitive to listeners. These included songs that referenced violence, such as Soundgarden's "Blow Up the Outside World," as well as songs that referenced falling, jumping, or flying. Most bands only had one or two songs targeted, but others had more songs pulled. For example, all of Rage Against the Machine's songs were on the list. Participation in pulling these songs was voluntary for radio stations, but many complied. As a result of this, Rage Against the Machine as well as other bands, such as

Slayer, laid low for a while. Slipknot, however, stood their ground and continued to tour and give fans an outlet from the tragedy. Taylor spoke about metal being constantly blamed for bad things that happen in society, saying,

Anything bad that happens, we're the focal point. It's just not fair. It spits in the face of everything we try to do, which is give an outlet for people who don't have that outlet. Take the violence some people have the propensity for, and make it positive. Give them the outlet to let [it] go.[48]

In 2004, Slipknot's third major-label album was released. Called *Vol. 3: The Subliminal Verses*, it truly showed off each member's strengths and the hard work they put into the creation of the album. It included songs such as "Pulse of the Maggots," "Duality," "Before I Forget," and "Vermilion." This album was another win for the band, as it went to number 2 on the Billboard charts and was certified platinum less than year after its release date. Slipknot even won a Best Metal Performance Grammy Award for "Before I Forget" in 2005. As of 2018, this is the band's only win out of 10 nominations. However, as Slipknot fans know well, a Grammy is not needed to tell them that Slipknot puts out solid, high-quality music.

Vol. 3: The Subliminal Verses was followed by *All Hope Is Gone* in 2008. The album, which was also certified platinum, was their first to sit at number 1 on the Billboard charts. The same year, they participated in the first *Mayhem Festival* tour with Disturbed. However, this album is also well-known for another reason, which is that it is the last album with bassist Paul Gray. In 2010, the band as well as their fans received tragic news about Gray's death from a drug overdose. The band decided to continue on without him, releasing their next album four years later. During this time, drummer Joey Jordison was released from the band due to what they thought were drug issues—he had to be carried onstage and could not play the drums.

Slipknot is known for putting out strong albums that showcase each member's strengths. Fans have also been drawn to the unique style of the band, shown in the masks worn by its members.

GRAMMY AWARDS CONTROVERSY

In 2015, the metal world was enraged and shocked by who won the Grammy for Best Metal Performance, just as it had been in 1989 when Jethro Tull won. The nominees included choices such as Anthrax, Mastodon, Motörhead, and Slipknot. However, the award went to Tenacious D—a comedy music act fronted by actors Jack Black and Kyle Gass that, like Jethro Tull, has never been considered metal. This immediately enraged metal fans, and some of them took to the internet to express their feelings. One of these people, Kim Kelly, wrote on Vice, "To have chosen Jack Black and Kyle Gass as a representation of what the music industry considers the pinnacle of the genre's achievement for the year is to say that the most they expect from heavy metal (and the people who love it) is a dumb, crude, laughable piece of [music]."[1]

More controversy came in 2018, when Avenged Sevenfold was nominated for Best Rock Song. The band was pleased they were in the rock category rather than metal because that award is typically televised. In addition, it was the band's first Grammy nomination. However, the band boycotted the Grammy Awards after it was announced that none of the rock awards were going to be televised either. Avenged Sevenfold's front man, M. Shadows, said,

If you're getting a metal award, they don't actually televise it. So, no one sees it; it doesn't move the needle [on the metaphorical gauge of public interest] at all. I think the GRAMMYs have to get that right. When you look at metal, it's probably one of the healthiest genres when you look at it in a worldwide perspective. Every single country listens to metal, and whether it's mainstream or not is irrelevant. People will watch your program if you're giving awards to bands that deserve it and it's actually on TV and help those bands push the needle forward ... It helps everybody when the bands can get bigger. So, the metal award is still a problem, because literally no one is going to see those bands or know that they're nominated, and that's an issue.[2]

1. Kim Kelly, "This Is Why It's Stupid Tenacious D Won the Grammy for Best Metal Performance," Vice, February 8, 2015. noisey.vice.com/en_us/article/r3zn89/tenacious-d-grammy-best-metal.

2. Quoted in Erica Banas, "Another GRAMMY Telecast, Another Snub For Rock Fans," WROR, January 26, 2018. wror.com/2018/01/26/another-grammy-telecast-another-snub-rock-fans/.

In 2016, Jordison gave an interview in which he expressed frustration that his bandmates had believed he was taking drugs; he revealed that he was actually suffering from a form of multiple sclerosis, a nerve disease that made it extremely hard for him to walk or play music.

Slipknot's follow-up to *All Hope Is Gone* was much more personal and was titled *.5: The Gray Chapter*. It was their second album to reach number 1 on the Billboard charts and included the song "Goodbye," which was written about Gray's death. Taylor said,

> I wrote that song about the day Paul died. I was sitting in my house, and it was the first time the whole band hadn't been in the house because Paul wasn't there. It was a heavy moment for me. We were all sitting in my basement looking at each other, and it was the thickest kind of silence. So quiet you can't ignore it. Finally we started to help each other let loose a little bit, there was a lot of crying, we tried to laugh as much as we could just because we were so thrown for a … loop we didn't know what to do.[49]

The day after Gray died, the band held a press conference in which they stressed that Gray was the essence of the band, one of the original members, and they would not be where they are today without him.

Avenged Sevenfold

Avenged Sevenfold, also known as A7X, is one of the most successful metal bands; they have sold more than 8 million total copies of their seven albums as of 2018. Avenged Sevenfold was formed in 1999 by singer M. Shadows (Matthew Sanders) and guitarist Zacky Vengeance (Zachary Baker). Later, bassist Johnny Christ (Jonathan Seward), guitarist Synyster Gates (Brian Haner Jr.), and The Rev, also known as The Reverend Tholomew Plague (Jimmy Sullivan) were added to the band. Each band member has incredible talent; their live shows are astounding, and they fully put on a show for fans. Their shows have included a large three-dimensional deathbat that takes up the entire stage, a deathbed with a crown and sword behind the drum set, and plenty of fire.

Avenged Sevenfold had characteristics of metalcore music before the style became extremely mainstream, and this is evident in their early releases. They released the album *Sounding the Seventh Trumpet* in 2001 with indie label Good Life Recordings, then signed with Hopeless Records the following year. Hopeless Records re-released *Sounding the Seventh Trumpet*, which was followed by the more aggressive and focused album *Waking the Fallen*, which reached number 12 on the Billboard Independent Albums chart and featured songs such as "Unholy Confessions" and "I Won't See You Tonight" parts one and two. During this time, the band also came up with the deathbat logo they still use today, much like Iron Maiden's mascot. It is not just coincidence—M. Shadows stated in a 2018 interview that one of their largest influences is Iron Maiden because of their style of thrash, storytelling, melody, and speed. He also said Avenged Sevenfold was influenced by Metallica, Slayer, Megadeth, and even the Beatles.

Reaching number 12 on the Billboard chart was an achievement for the band, but their third album, *City of Evil*, was when they broke through and really grabbed people's attention. With this major-label album through Warner Brothers Records, the band broke away from the screaming vocals that are present on their first two albums. The reasoning behind this was partially because it was what they wanted to do and partially because M. Shadows had just had surgery to remove a blood vessel from his vocal cords that would flare up, resulting in his throat closing up. Throat problems are common for metal vocalists because screaming puts great strain on the vocal cords. In summer 2018, the band had to cancel their entire tour due to a blister on M. Shadows's vocal folds, leaving him unable to sing. Even though M. Shadows did not scream vocals as he had on previous albums, *City of Evil* still has a number of epic songs, such as "Sidewinder," "The Wicked End," and "Betrayed," which is about the death of Dimebag Darrell. While the entire album shows off the musicianship of the band, songs such as "Seize the Day," "Bat Country," and "Beast and the Harlot" were especially successful for the band.

Two years later, their popularity soared even more with the release of their self-titled album. This album is the first to feature each band member's voice, including The Rev's vocals on the chorus of "Critical Acclaim." *Avenged Sevenfold* went to number 4 on the Billboard album charts and included songs such as "Almost Easy," "A Little Piece of Heaven," and "Afterlife." While each band member is incredibly talented, the dual-guitar attack of Zacky Vengeance and Synyster Gates is something that continues to awe fans. This is especially evident on "Afterlife," a song written entirely by The Rev, which features a string orchestra as well as a jaw-dropping, blisteringly fast guitar solo courtesy of Synyster Gates. Synyster Gates also created an extremely fast guitar solo for "Scream." He said, "The solo is the hardest solo to

*The Rev had incredible talent that is still legendary among fans.
He is shown here with his equally legendary drum kit.*

play because it's all picked; it may sound like it's something else, but it's all picked, it's all [these] fast, ridiculous triplets."[50]

The guitar skills of Synyster Gates and Zacky Vengeance are incredible, and another member had rare talent that was revered by fans. Drummer Jimmy "The Rev" Sullivan was part of what made Avenged Sevenfold shows fun to watch. With each show, he displayed not only talent but also pure enthusiasm for what he was doing. Avenged Sevenfold's music is known for being incredibly fast and demanding on the members. In a 2006

review, *Modern Drummer* magazine wrote that The Rev gave "the crowd a lot to watch while plowing his way through seriously demanding music. He pulls off complex hand-foot combinations with metronomic precision at wickedly fast tempos, and he does it all while twirling his sticks. He slashes and slices at his kit, his long arms flying at full extension, first this way, then that."[51] The Rev began playing drums at a young age, astounding people with his talent even then. Years later, with Avenged Sevenfold, he fit well with the band's sound and had special techniques along with a double

Avenged Sevenfold is one of the most successful bands in metal. They continue to release powerful, unique albums and put on awe-inspiring live shows.

bass drum kit.

The success of 2007's self-titled album prompted the band to start writing their next album. However, on December 28, 2009, everything changed for the band and their fan base when The Rev died of a drug overdose. The band continued writing their next album, *Nightmare*, but acknowledged that they did not know what the future would hold. Released in 2010, the absence of The Rev is noticeable throughout the album, starting with the cover itself. It features a gravestone with the word "Forever" on it, with the letters "REV" larger than the others. Additionally, the album features the song "So Far Away," which was a tribute to The Rev.

Despite such a huge loss to the

THE RISE AND FALL OF MAYHEM FESTIVAL

Along with *Ozzfest*, *Mayhem Festival* was a must-see festival for metal fans.. In fact, *Mayhem Festival* was so popular that it overshadowed *Ozzfest*'s presence, shrinking *Ozzfest* from a multi-city tour to just one show. Throughout the eight years of the *Mayhem Festival*, acts such as Slipknot, Disturbed, Slayer, Marilyn Manson, Rob Zombie, Megadeth, and Avenged Sevenfold headlined tours.

However, the 2015 festival ended up being the last. That year, the festival experienced poor ticket sales, but even worse, the cofounder of the festival, Kevin Lyman, insulted metal. This resulted in extreme backlash from the headliners and even from bands who were not on the festival lineup, such as Lamb of God. In his original statement about why the festival might soon end for good, Lyman made logical arguments, such as the finances of putting on a tour; he later expanded on these statements in a follow-up apology statement. However, Lyman also said things that he did not address in the apology statement—such as his statement about female fans of metal. Lyman said, "What happened was metal chased girls away because what happened was metal aged ... Metal got gray, bald and fat. And metal was about danger. When you went to a metal show, it was dudes onstage; there was some danger in it."[1] However, plenty of women listen to metal on a daily basis, go to metal shows frequently, write books about metal, and actually play in metal bands. Women get involved in the metal scene because of pure enjoyment of the music, not because of the physical looks of the people playing it. Lamb of God's Randy Blythe took to social media to respond to Lyman's comment, noting that the metal scene is doing fine and that plenty of women attend his shows. Blythe's response was what many people, especially women, were thinking, but his popularity and visibility gave his comments more exposure.

1. Quoted in Robert Pasbani, "MAYHEM FEST May Go Away Due to Lack of Headliner; Founder Calls Metal 'Gray, Bald & Fat,'" Metal Injection, July 8, 2015. www.metalinjection.net/latest-news/drama/mayhem-fest-may-go-away-due-to-lack-of-headliner-founder-calls-metal-gray-bald-fat.

band and music world, Avenged Sevenfold decided to carry on, adding Arin Ilejay as drummer in 2011. He was with the band throughout the next album, *Hail to the King*, which was released in 2013. Both *Nightmare* and *Hail to the King* hit number 1 on the Billboard album chart, and the band continued to tour.

In 2014, Ilejay was released from the band and was replaced with Brooks Wackerman. In 2016, the band surprised fans by releasing their next album, *The Stage*, with no notice whatsoever that they were releasing it. They became the first band in history to pull this stunt and release the album in both physical and digital forms. The album was another success for Avenged Sevenfold, reaching number 3 on the Billboard album chart. The album, with its themes of artificial intelligence and science, was an ambitious release by the band and included a 15-minute song, "Exist," that included a cameo by astrophysicist Neil deGrasse Tyson reading a portion of one of his essays. For this album, the band researched the works of scientist Carl Sagan and entrepreneur Elon Musk. As the album progresses, the strength of the songs also progresses, resulting in an incredibly powerful, unique release. Following this album, the band embarked on tours with Metallica. Whatever the band continues to do in the future, their past album history suggests that new albums will continue to be out of the box and the accompanying tours will continue to astound fans in new ways.

In This Moment

In This Moment was formed in 2005 by Maria Brink and Chris Howorth. Brink has a powerful voice with a wide range that immediately grabs the listener's attention. In 2007, their debut album, *Beautiful Tragedy*, was released, and in this same year, they toured with *Ozzfest*, which gained exposure for the band. Following this album, they released their follow-up, *The Dream*, and toured with *Ozzfest* again in 2008. *The Dream* received positive reviews and was their first album to chart on the Billboard 200, landing at number 73.

In 2010, they released *A Star-Crossed Wasteland*, which spawned fan favorites such as "Into the Light" and "Forever." This album peaked even higher on the Billboard album charts, landing at number 40. In This Moment's following releases have charted even higher, and the band continues to grow and show their pure talent and musicianship. In 2012, their fourth album, *Blood*, was released, reaching number 15 on the Billboard album charts. Throughout this time, the band had lineup changes, but this album was just as strong as the previous ones. It includes chaotic songs such as "Beast Within," "Comanche," and "Blood" and shows off Brink's vocal power with chilling songs such as "The Blood Legion," "11:11," and "Scarlet." As Loudwire wrote in a review of the album *Ritual*, "Brink has an outstanding voice with a lot of power and texture, and when unleashed is a potent force."[52]

Two years after releasing *Blood*, their fifth album, *Black Widow*, was released, which peaked at number 8 on the Billboard chart. In 2017, *Ritual* was released and hit number 9 on the Billboard chart.

In This Moment creates powerful music fronted by Maria Brink's astounding voice.

The first full song on the album is the hit "Oh Lord," and *Ritual* also includes the song "Black Wedding," which features Rob Halford of Judas Priest. Throughout their career, In This Moment's music has evolved, and Brink's voice continues to astound fans, who eagerly await each new release.

The Future of Metal

Metal was created out of displeasure with current events and music that was not accurately portraying the complicated feelings of the time. This desire to do things differently created an entirely new genre of music, which bands continued to build on, creating new movements of metal that expanded the genre even further. Early pioneers of metal music, such as Black Sabbath and Judas Priest, opened the music industry up for the New Wave of British Heavy Metal, which expanded options for harder thrash metal bands such as the Big Four. Throughout its history, the genre has continued to surprise and shock listeners and non-listeners alike, creating controversy while splintering off into subgenres. With all these changes, metal has also proven one thing: It is not going away, and it is only continuing to evolve as each new band puts their own spin on things.

Notes

Introduction:
Vivaldi to Vietnam: Metal's Roots

1. Robert Walser, *Running with the Devil: Power, Gender, and Madness in Heavy Metal Music.* Hanover, NH: Wesleyan University Press, 1993, p. 103.
2. Mike McPadden, "6.66 Hot Points of the '80s Heavy Metal Satanic Panic," VH1 News, February 11, 2015. www.vh1.com/news/54726/remembering-the-80s-heavy-metal-satanic-panic/.
3. Robert Walser, "Heavy Metal," *Encyclopedia Britannica*, accessed on March 21, 2018. www.britannica.com/art/heavy-metal-music.
4. Walser, *Running with the Devil*, p. 103.

Chapter One:
Evolution of Early Metal

5. "A Brief History of Metal," Massachusetts Institute of Technology: Heavy Metal 101, accessed on March 24, 2018. metal.mit.edu/brief-history-metal.
6. David Konow, *Bang Your Head: The Rise and Fall of Heavy Metal.* New York, NY: Three Rivers Press, 2002, pp. 3–4.
7. Konow, *Bang Your Head*, p. 6.
8. Konow, *Bang Your Head*, p. 7.
9. Konow, *Bang Your Head*, p. 7.
10. Quoted in Konow, *Bang Your Head*, p. 7.
11. Quoted in Konow, *Bang Your Head*, p. 11.
12. Konow, *Bang Your Head*, p. 25.
13. Konow, *Bang Your Head*, p. 26.
14. Ian Christe, *Sound of the Beast: The Complete Headbanging History of Heavy Metal.* New York, NY: HarperEntertainment, 2003, p. 20.
15. Christe, *Sound of the Beast*, p. 20.
16. Quoted in Christe, *Sound of the Beast*, pp. 20–21.

17. Quoted in Mike McPadden, "6.66 Hot Points."
18. Simon Reynolds, "Alice Cooper: 'Rock Music was Looking for a Villain,'" *The Guardian*, June 12, 2014. www.theguardian.com/music/2014/jun/12/alice-cooper-i-realised-rock-needed-a-villain-super-duper-alice-cooper-documentary.
19. Quoted in Konow, *Bang Your Head*, p. 34.

Chapter Two:
New Wave of British Heavy Metal
20. Quoted in Christe, *Sound of the Beast*, pp. 67.
21. "Rime of the Ancient Mariner," track 8 on Iron Maiden, *Powerslave*. Capitol, 1984.
22. "Rime of the Ancient Mariner," track 8 on Iron Maiden, *Powerslave*.
23. Konow, *Bang Your Head*, p. 160.

Chapter Three:
The Big Four
24. Deena Weinstein, *Heavy Metal: The Music and Its Culture*. Cambridge, MA: Da Capo Press, 2000, p. 49.
25. Weinstein, *Heavy Metal*, p. 50.
26. Quoted in "EXODUS Singer Says 'Big Four' of Thrash Metal Is Really 'the Big One and the Other Three,'" Blabbermouth, October 18, 2014. www.blabbermouth.net/news/exodus-singer-says-big-four-of-thrash-metal-is-really-the-big-one-and-the-other-three/.
27. Quoted in "EXODUS Singer Says 'Big Four' of Thrash Metal Is Really 'the Big One and the Other Three,'" Blabbermouth.
28. Quoted in "EXODUS Singer Says 'Big Four' of Thrash Metal Is Really 'the Big One and the Other Three,'" Blabbermouth.
29. Konow, *Bang Your Head*, p. 148.
30. Konow, *Bang Your Head*, p. 149.
31. Konow, *Bang Your Head*, p. 149.
32. "History," Metallica.com, accessed on April 20, 2018. www.metallica.com/band/history.
33. Steve Huey, "Slayer," AllMusic, accessed on April 21, 2018. www.allmusic.com/artist/slayer-mn0000022124/biography.
34. Huey, "Slayer."

35. Kim Kelly, "This Is Why It's Stupid Tenacious D Won the Grammy for Best Metal Performance," Vice, February 8, 2015. noisey.vice.com/en_us/article/r3zn89/tenacious-d-grammy-best-metal.

36. Quoted in "CANNIBAL CORPSE: 'We Listen to SLAYER so Much that the Influence Is Probably Very Pervasive,'" Blabbermouth, November 18, 2009. www.blabbermouth.net/news/cannibal-corpse-we-listen-to-slayer-so-much-that-the-influence-is-probably-very-pervasive/.

37. Konow, *Bang Your Head*, p. 144.

Chapter Four:
Endless Controversy

38. Jason Birchmeier, "Pantera," AllMusic, accessed on April 28, 2018. www.allmusic.com/artist/pantera-mn0000005441/biography.

39. Aja Romano, "The History of Satanic Panic in the US—and Why It's not Over Yet," Vox, October 30, 2016. www.vox.com/2016/10/30/13413864/satanic-panic-ritual-abuse-history-explained.

40. Romano, "The History of Satanic Panic in the US—and Why It's not Over Yet."

41. Marilyn Manson, "Columbine: Whose Fault Is It?," *Rolling Stone*, June 24, 1999. www.rollingstone.com/culture/news/columbine-whose-fault-is-it-19990624.

42. Hank Shteamer, "Opeth's Mikael Akerfeldt: My 10 Favorite Metal Albums," *Rolling Stone*, July 26, 2017. www.rollingstone.com/music/lists/opeths-mikael-akerfeldt-my-10-favorite-metal-albums-w493840.

43. Chris Dick, "Biography," Opeth.com, accessed on April 29, 2018. www.opeth.com/bio.

44. "Concepts," Chthonic.com, accessed on April 29, 2018. www.chthonic.tw/2009/en/concept_us.php.

Chapter Five:
Metal Today

45. "Lip Gloss and Black," track 10 on Atreyu, *Suicide Notes and Butterfly Kisses*. Victory, 2002.

46. John Hill, "Rank Your Records: Slipknot's Corey Taylor Rates 20 Years' Worth of Mayhem," Vice, April 16, 2015. noisey.vice.com/en_us/article/65zg3k/rank-your-records-slipknot-corey-taylor.

47. Quoted in Hill, "Rank Your Records."

48. Quoted in Hill, "Rank Your Records."

49. Quoted in Hill, "Rank Your Records."

50. Rafa Alcantara, dir., *The Making of* Avenged Sevenfold. Warner Brothers Records, 2007, MVI DVD.

51. Michael Parillo, "James 'The Rev' Sullivan," *Modern Drummer*, October 2006. www.moderndrummer.com/2009/12/james-the-rev-sullivan/.

52. Chad Bowar, "In This Moment, 'Ritual'—Album Review," Loudwire, July 21, 2017. loudwire.com/in-this-moment-ritual-album-review/.

Essential
Albums

Publisher's note: Some albums may contain strong language or explicit content.

Anthrax
Fistful of Metal (1984)

Atreyu
A Death-Grip on Yesterday (2006)

Avenged Sevenfold
The Stage (2016)
Waking the Fallen (2003)

Black Sabbath
Black Sabbath (1970)
Paranoid (1970)

Chthonic
Seediq Bale (2005)

In This Moment
Blood (2012)
Ritual (2017)

Iron Maiden
The Number of the Beast (1982)

Judas Priest
British Steel (1980)
Screaming for Vengeance (1982)

Lacuna Coil
Broken Crown Halo (2014)
Comalies (2002)
Delirium (2016)

Metallica
Master of Puppets (1986)
Metallica (1991)

Opeth
Blackwater Park (2001)

Ozzy Osbourne
Black Rain (2007)
Blizzard of Ozz (1981)

Pantera
Vulgar Display of Power (1992)

Rob Zombie
Hellbilly Deluxe (1998)

Slipknot
Iowa (2001)
Slipknot (1999)
Vol. 3: The Subliminal Verses (2004)

For More
Information

Books

Christe, Ian. *Sound of the Beast: The Complete Headbanging History of Heavy Metal.* New York, NY: HarperEntertainment, 2003.
> Christe's book is a must-read for metal fans and includes plenty of information about the first 30 years of metal music. Each chapter includes a list of essential albums that came out during the time period being discussed, and the book also includes more than 100 interviews with members of bands such as Judas Priest, Metallica, and more.

Konow, David. *Bang Your Head: The Rise and Fall of Heavy Metal.* New York, NY: Three Rivers Press, 2002.
> This book is a complete history of heavy metal that Konow spent years working on by interviewing the major players, both past and present, in the metal scene.

Slagel, Brian, and Mark Eglinton. *For the Sake of Heaviness: The History of Metal Blade Records.* Los Angeles, CA: BMG Books, 2017.
> Brian Slagel and Metal Blade Records were very influential in metal music. This book tells the story of the record company, provides the advice Slagel gave bands such as Mötley Crüe, and includes interviews with influential musicians.

Wiederhorn, Jon, and Katherine Turman. *Louder Than Hell: The Definitive Oral History of Metal.* New York, NY: It Books, 2013.
> This book includes hundreds of interviews with musicians in the metal scene, providing a thorough history of the genre from those who were involved in its creation.

Websites

Blabbermouth
www.blabbermouth.net

Blabbermouth's website includes the latest news articles on metal musicians along with album reviews.

Loudwire
loudwire.com

This website includes current news on metal and rock musicians as well as information on new and old albums and songs musicians have released.

Metal Injection
www.metalinjection.net

Metal Injection has up-to-date information on musicians, tour dates, upcoming music, exclusive video interviews, and podcasts.

Rolling Stone
www.rollingstone.com

Rolling Stone magazine's website includes biographies of musicians in the metal scene, along with current and archived articles.

Index

Picture
Credits

Cover (main) Peter Gudella/Shutterstock.com; cover (background), back cover, pp. 3–4, 6, 10, 28, 42, 59, 75, 93, 97, 98, 100, 103–104 Mathew Tucciarone/Shutterstock.com; pp. 7, 65 Mark Weiss/Getty Images; p. 8 Fine Art Images/Heritage Images/Getty Images; p. 13 Ellen Poppinga—K & K/Redferns/Getty Images; p. 15 Michael Ochs Archives/Getty Images; pp. 17, 19, 45 Fin Costello/Redferns/Getty Images; p. 22 Laura Levine/Images/Getty Images; p. 25 Keystone/Getty Images; p. 29 Kevin Winter/Getty Images for Live Nation; p. 33 Martin Philbey/Redferns/Getty Images; p. 34 George Wilkes/Hulton Archive/Getty Images; p. 36 C Brandon/Redferns/Getty Images; p. 39 Chris Walter/WireImage/Getty Images; p. 43 Marko Ristic ZT/Shutterstock.com; p. 49 Mauricio Santana/WireImage/Getty Images; p. 51 Annabel Staff/Redferns/Getty Images; p. 53 Waring Abbott/Getty Images; p. 55 Scott Eisen/Getty Images for Warner Bros.; pp. 57, 87 Ethan Miller/Getty Images; p. 61 Paul Natkin/WireImage/Getty Images; p. 62 Phillip Faraone/Getty Images for Sundance Film Festival; p. 69 Santiago Bluguermann/LatinContent/Getty Images; pp. 70, 83 Mick Hutson/Redferns/Getty Images; p. 73 SAM YEH/AFP/Getty Images; p. 76 Frazer Harrison/Getty Images; p. 79 ZUMA Press, Inc./Alamy Stock Photo; p. 88 Rebecca Sapp/WireImage for The Recording Academy/Getty Images; p. 91 Jeremy Saffer/Metal Hammer Magazine via Getty Images.

About
the Author

Nicole Horning has written a number of books for children. She holds a bachelor's degree in English and a master's degree in special education from D'Youville College in Buffalo, New York. Nicole lives in Western New York with her cats, Khaleesi and Evie. She reads, writes, and attends metal concerts in her free time.